He was the
she was gla~~~

Tessa pulled back the gun and licked her lips to make the tingling go away. The past had slammed into her, knocking the breath out of her the moment she'd seen him. The power he had over her. scared her spitless, so she'd gone on the offensive and attacked him. The only other choice she had was to collapse into his arms, and she couldn't do that. She couldn't give him a toehold— nothing. If she did, he would take everything and leave her empty again.

They were so close, she could smell his tangy scent, feel his breath feather her cheek. She crossed her arms tightly so she wouldn't reach out to him in the darkness....

He was the devil's own—but
she was glad he'd come.

ROGUE
SOLDIER
DANA MARTON

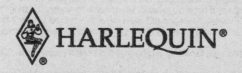

TORONTO • NEW YORK • LONDON
AMSTERDAM • PARIS • SYDNEY • HAMBURG
STOCKHOLM • ATHENS • TOKYO • MILAN • MADRID
PRAGUE • WARSAW • BUDAPEST • AUCKLAND

This book is dedicated to Allison Lyons
for all her wonderful help.

With many thanks to Anita Staley and Jenel Looney
for their help and support. And with much appreciation to
Carmen Bydalek, Carla Gingrich, Jean Fassler and Rose Notti
of Alaska for setting me straight on a number of details. Many
thanks as well to the Nome Public Library.

ISBN 0-373-88676-4

ROGUE SOLDIER

Copyright © 2006 by Dana Marton

This edition published by arrangement with Harlequin Books S.A.

® and TM are trademarks of the publisher. Trademarks indicated with
® are registered in the United States Patent and Trademark Office, the
Canadian Trade Marks Office and in other countries.

www.eHarlequin.com

Printed in U.S.A.

ABOUT THE AUTHOR

Dana Marton lives near Wilmington, Delaware. She has been an avid reader since childhood and has a master's degree in writing popular fiction. When not writing, she can be found either in her garden or her home library. For more information on the author and her other novels, please visit her Web site at www.danamarton.com.

She would love to hear from her readers via e-mail: DanaMarton@yahoo.com.

Books by Dana Marton

HARLEQUIN INTRIGUE
806—SHADOW SOLDIER
821—SECRET SOLDIER
859—THE SHEIK'S SAFETY
875—CAMOUFLAGE HEART
902—ROGUE SOLDIER

CAST OF CHARACTERS

Mike McNair—Member of SDDU, a top-secret military group. When he finds out that the only woman he's ever loved is kidnapped, he goes AWOL to rush to Alaska and rescue her.

Tessa Nielsen—Tessa does not appreciate Mike's return. But as they fight for their lives, she begins to wonder just how much he's changed over the last few years.

SDDU—Special Designation Defense Unit. A top secret military team established to fight terrorism. Its existence is known only by a select few. Members are recruited from the best of the best, SEALs, FBI and CIA agents, elite military groups.

Brady Marshall—Mike's old nemesis at the CIA. But what does he have to do with Tessa's kidnapping?

Tommy Cattaro—A.K.A. Shorty. He used to be one of Mike's best friends and is now the only person who can help Mike and Tessa out of this mess.

Tsernyakov—An elusive arms dealer, wanted on three continents. Although results of his work are well known to the authorities, his identity isn't.

Colonel Wilson—Mike's boss. He's the leader of the SDDU, reporting straight to the Homeland Security Secretary.

Chapter One

Of all the stupid things he'd done in his life, this might take the cake. He didn't even know for sure that she was still alive. All he had to go by was a partial sentence in a two-page report he wasn't supposed to have seen: "team was unable to recover the second body." Not exactly a beacon of hope, considering that the other researcher had been found half-eaten by bears.

Mike McNair crept across the snow, each step placed with care. He didn't want to crunch the icy mess underfoot. The sled dogs were upwind so they couldn't smell him. He had to make sure they didn't hear him, either, now that the squalls had died down and the afternoon was shrouded in the absolute silence that existed only in the farthest reaches of the world.

The enemy was inside, all six of the men. He hoped Tessa was with them.

A gun would have come in handy under the circumstances, but his rifle lay in the snow on the bottom of an inaccessible ravine, next to his backpack of supplies. It could have been worse—he could have been killed when the ledge gave way under him.

He hadn't been. He'd made it, and he would get Tessa back, no matter what it took. Then he would do the best damn fast-talking he'd ever done in his life and convince the Colonel to overlook this little adventure.

Fat chance of that. Wake up, buddy, and smell the court-martial.

People didn't go AWOL from the SDDU every day. The Special Designation Defense Unit, a top-secret military team founded only five years ago, consisted of elite soldiers, the best of the best.

Mike moved forward in a crouch, inch by inch until he reached the silvery white, steel-reinforced mobile research vehicle that was designed to house two scientists and their lab equipment and was strong enough to withstand a polar bear attack. Snow partially obscured the CRREL logo on the side—Cold Regions Research and Engineering Laboratory.

The bitter cold made his eyes water. Couldn't be more than twenty degrees this morning. The pilot who had dropped him in three days ago told him it was the best weather they'd seen at this time of the year in a long time. He hoped Tessa and he would be out of here before the temperature dropped.

He blinked as he turned and walked back to the edge of the Alaskan alders where he'd trampled the snow into an unrecognizable array of tracks earlier. Careful to place his boots exactly in the first set of prints that led to the vehicle, he returned to it and looked back to examine his handiwork—footwork, really. It looked good.

To anyone but the most trained observer, the two sets of tracks looked like someone had come over to the trailer, then gone back to the woods. He counted on the element of surprise, that the men would focus on finding out who was out there spying on them, and wouldn't notice that the tracks leading to the vehicle were a millimeter or two deeper than the ones leading away.

He reached into his pocket and pulled out the greasy paper he had collected that afternoon, along with a handful of other garbage the wind had blown from the trailer into the grove of trees. He rolled everything together then lit the end with one of his few remaining waterproof matches and held the smoking mess up to the vent hole.

No sound came from inside.

If Tessa was alive and unharmed, he would be content to take her and leave the men to the CIA. If she'd been hurt in any way, all bets were off.

A couple of minutes passed before he heard the door slam open on the other side. Play time. He leaped around the corner and dove under the vehicle, rolled to the middle. Four pairs of legs came around in fur boots.

"Where's the fire?"

"Ja nye znau." The response came in Russian. *I don't know.*

The boots stopped at his tracks.

"What the hell is this?"

The Russian called something back to the men in the trailer, then the four headed off toward the woods.

Mike ducked out on the other side, pulled his white parka over as much of his face as he could and banged on the door.

"Pahchemu tu—"

The door opened, and his mind registered the two men inside, Tessa tied up on the floor in the corner. She had a dark bruise on her face. And just like that, his plan of not doing more damage than necessary to her captors was forgotten.

The man standing in the doorway didn't have a chance to finish his sentence.

Mike crushed the guy's windpipe with one well-aimed strike a split second before the other man went for his gun and he had to jump him. He brought the guy down, shoved his index finger behind the trigger to make sure the weapon couldn't be discharged. He didn't want the others coming back in a hurry.

"Who the hell are you?" The man was gasping for air, his voice hoarse but recognizably American.

At least one of the four outside was a local boy, too. A joint operation? None of it made any sense. The man pulled a knife from somewhere with his free hand, but Mike finally got a good grip on the guy's head and heaved. The neck broke with a small pop, like cracking knuckles.

He paused to listen for anyone coming from outside, then a second later he was pulling the rags out of Tessa's mouth. She swallowed, ran her tongue over her dry lips, pushing her bound hands toward him.

"I should have gotten here sooner, honey. Are you all right?" He crushed her to his chest for a heart-stopping moment. She was alive. He hadn't been too late. *She was alive.*

He set her away to look at her and free her from the ropes. They had to get out of here fast.

"You bastard," was the first thing she said to him, her voice as hard as her eyes.

He stared at her for a second, a little hurt by the obvious anger on her face. Hell, she wasn't still mad at him, was she?

"Good to see you, too, hon. If I get these ropes off, you're not gonna hit me, are you?" He was cutting as he spoke. They didn't have any time to waste.

Tessa didn't seem to realize that. The second her hands were free, she socked him in the jaw with full force.

He teetered back. "Damn. What was that for?"

But she was already collecting the two rifles from the dead men and shrugging into a parka. Then she was out the door.

The woman moved fast.

He rushed after her, scanning the woods, but saw no sign of the men. They were probably searching for him farther in the forest. With a little luck, they'd keep at it for a while.

He caught up with Tessa by the pair of sleds—one metal, one wood—two crates on each. He figured explosives, from what he'd seen in that report. The dogs were harnessed and ready to go, jumping and yipping as they greeted her, but she silenced them quickly. She got on the metal sled, and he went to cut the leather harness on the other.

What the hell?

Her dogs were moving, leaning into the work. The sled broke loose of its snow bed with a jerk then slid forward smoothly. She meant to leave without him.

He had to run to jump on. "Come on, you can't still be mad at me." He shoved off one of the crates to make room for himself, and almost tipped the sled, sending the dogs into momentary disarray.

"Haa!" She snapped the whip above the animals' heads, her ice-blue eyes locked onto his face.

She looked exactly as he'd remembered her—magnificent with her generous lips and all that red hair escaping from her hood. The sight of her was like a sharp elbow in the chest.

Damn, he should have looked her up sooner.

"I went past mad a couple of years back, McNair. I'd just as soon shoot you as look at you."

She wasn't kidding. The fierce emotion on her face would have knocked a lesser man on his ass. Where had that come from? He hung on as the dogs picked up speed.

"Could we—" The rapid gunfire coming from the woods cut him off.

She tossed him one of the rifles. "Make yourself useful."

He did, spraying the edge of the forest. A moment of silence passed before response came.

They were out in the open, no place to take cover, and if he was correct, they were sharing the sled with some serious explosives—a hell of a target. He moved to shove the second crate off, then stopped. They were going pretty fast now. If he tipped the sled, if the dogs got tangled—if they slowed at all—they were as good as dead.

They would only have to make it the next few hundred feet to be out of range. If the men were stupid enough to leave the cover of the woods and come after them, he could pick them off one by one.

"Haa!" Tessa urged the dogs faster, and they gave her everything they had as if sensing the humans' desperation.

Bullets sprayed the snow around them, sending up powdery puffs of white. Just a little more. He did his best to get the men, but it was hard to take out people he couldn't see. All he could do was aim in the general direction where he figured the men were hiding behind trees and snow-drifts.

Then he glimpsed one who stepped out too far, and took aim, squeezing off a round at the same time as the man. Mike watched him fold slowly onto the snow as he heard a loud yelp from one of the dogs and the sled jerked sharply, the huskies slowing and tangling the line.

Which dog? He was in the snow on his feet, ignoring the bullets that kept coming. It was the black female husky with the light stripe across her shoulders—red spread on her hind leg, staining the snow.

He grabbed the dog and sliced the

leather that bound her to the harness, picked her up and jumped on the sled with her on his lap.

"Haa!" Tessa yelled to the rest, straightening the line.

The dogs listened to her and picked up speed again.

"That's Sasha. How's she doing?"

The dog yipped at him as he probed around the wound. "Easy, girl. I'm going to take care of you. Nothing to worry about." He talked to her in a soothing voice, petting her, allowing her time to get used to his scent. "Went clear through," he said to Tessa. At least they didn't have to worry about the bullet.

He let the dog lick the wound for a few seconds before he pushed her head away and slid his scarf off his neck to use as a bandage. He barely got it tied when the dog bent to pull it off.

"Sasha." Tessa's voice was firm.

The dog stopped pulling at the scarf, but was now trying to squirm out of his hold and get off the sled.

"Stay," Tessa said.

And Sasha finally lay her head on his lap with a pitiful whine of protest. Man, he felt bad for her. That bullet had been meant for him.

"Take it easy, girl. You'll be fine." He scratched her behind the ear.

The sled flew over the snow. They were out of firing range, but the men were still shooting, wasting bullets. He pressed his palm against Sasha's wound, hoping the pressure would stop the bleeding.

"How bad?" Tessa asked.

"She'll live if we don't run into any more trouble and can get help soon."

Tessa nodded and kept a good pace, calling to the dogs to spur them on, ignoring him for the next couple of miles.

"Where is your base camp?" She switched to a lower pace once the huskies tired.

"I don't have one."

"Your supplies?"

He shook his head, annoyed that he was embarrassed. He had tracked her down in the middle of the Alaskan wilderness, rescued her from a group of terrorists.

How in hell did she manage to make him feel as if that were insufficient?

"So you came to get me because you didn't want to starve and freeze alone?" She flashed him a look of contempt as only Tessa could.

God, she was gorgeous.

"They would have killed you." He rubbed Sasha behind the ears.

"Did it occur to you that I might have had a plan?"

No it hadn't. He'd heard that her research station had been attacked by some nutcases who were planning to blow up a chunk of the Alaskan pipeline, and he'd rushed after her against explicit orders that the SDDU was to stay out of this one since the CIA was handling the case.

He'd been lucky to dig up as much information as he had. He'd never seen a case more hushed up. The Colonel about had a stroke when Mike had asked to be allowed to get involved whether the CIA wanted him or not. Apparently, the agency's director had been making a bid to bring the SDDU under his supervision. One wrong move from anyone in the Special Designation Defense Unit, and the whole group could cease to exist as they knew it.

A fat snowflake floated onto his nose, then more and more came, chasing each other down from the endless gray sky. For once he didn't mind. Snow would cover their tracks.

"So what was your plan?" He pulled his hood closer to his stinging cheeks, as the wind picked up and the clouds began dumping their loads in earnest, reducing visibility to a few yards. He shifted to shield Sasha from the elements as much as he could.

"Have them drive around in circles until fuel ran out, then take the dog teams and leave them stranded," she said.

"Could have worked."

"Whoa!" She pulled on the reins and brought the team to a slow halt. "Let's give them a little rest." She stepped off the back runners and came straight to Sasha, knelt in the snow and buried her face in the dog's fur, murmuring words of reassurance he couldn't understand.

"Come on, let me see you," she said as she lifted the dog off his lap and took her into her arms. "You're such a good dog."

She checked the bandage, and he was happy to see no fresh blood gush forth when she pulled up the edge.

"Why don't you set that up?" She nodded toward the jumble of furs he'd been sitting on.

"They'll catch up with us."

"Not yet. You cut the harness on the other sled. None of them can mush dogs worth anything, anyway. The weather is turning for the worse. We're better off letting the huskies rest now so they'll be ready to cover serious ground when the snow clears out."

She made sense. He yanked at the furs. They were all connected, a patchwork that made a good-size cover, at least ten by ten or so, the large polar bear fur in the middle surrounded by wolf pelts. He spread it and crawled under it, held up one end to let her in when she came back with the dogs. The shelter was pretty low, supported by their heads as they sat on the sled, uncomfortable.

He took one of the rifles and jammed it upright into the front of the sled, using it as makeshift tent pole. One of the dogs growled at him when he stepped too close.

"They'll get used to you," she said.

He couldn't resist needling her. "Scared to be alone with me? I thought these puppies could handle the cold."

"They can. They're here to keep us warm." She didn't rise to the bait.

Well, what do you know? She had matured.

Man, things had changed. For one, three years ago they sure hadn't needed a dog team for heat. Their wild and crazy escapades had been plenty hot.

Obviously, she didn't feel that way about him anymore. Walking out on him with the parting words "Drop dead" should have given him a clue.

He'd been hoping for a warmer reunion, had entertained some fantasies while sleeping in the snow on the way to her—

about Tessa Nielsen jumping into his arms in gratitude. Of course, the woman never could appreciate a good rescue. He should have remembered that.

Sasha slid from between them, abandoning the humans for her canine family. Thank God her injury wasn't worse.

"Reminds me of one of Grandpa Fergus's stories about a whole winter he spent in a cave in the highlands," he said.

She didn't respond.

She was mad all right. She used to love his Grandpa Fergus stories.

They huddled in the dark silence of the tent. He assessed their situation and tried to come up with a workable plan, but it wasn't easy with Tessa right next to him.

He could have recognized her by scent alone. She'd never been one for perfumes, but she had her own unique feminine essence that made him think of soft warm places and the way she would taste if he pressed his lips against her neck just below her ear. The way her eyes would glaze over if he dragged his day-old stubble over that sensitive patch of skin.

"So you and this Dr. Lippman, living out on the snowfields for months at a time, were…" He voiced the question that had been bugging him for days.

Two dogs snapped at each other, and she recognized them from sound, called them by name and calmed them down before returning her attention to him.

"Lovers? Is that what you want to know?"

The idea hurt. Man, he was an idiot. What had he expected? A woman like Tessa had probably had a dozen lovers in the past three years. Hell, she could get anyone. "Never mind."

"We tried, but it didn't work. We were much better at being colleagues than being a couple."

Some of the tension seeped out of his shoulders. He held back the need to ask what exactly "tried" meant. He wished he could see her face, but it was pitch-dark, their makeshift tent smelling like eau-de-wet-dog.

He moved closer in the direction of her voice, and they bumped knees. She pulled away.

She didn't fool him, though. No way had she forgotten what they'd once had between them. She was probably hurt that he hadn't come after her before this. Hell, he would have, but he'd been on one overseas assignment after another.

He remembered every damn night they'd ever spent together—in detail. No time like the present to refresh her memory. He reached out and found her, cupped her face.

"I missed you," he whispered before lowering his mouth to hers.

Her lips were soft and warm, and he sank into the sensation awakening his body from head to toe. He tasted the corners, not wanting to push, even as he burned for the rest of her. Then he felt the barrel of a gun press against the soft spot under his chin.

"Get away from me, McNair," she said, her voice as cold as the gunmetal.

SHE HATED THE WAY her body responded to him still, like a dog to the voice of his master, panting and jumping with excitement. Mike

McNair did not control her. Not anymore. She'd worked hard to exile his memory and the emotions tangled up with it.

Tessa pulled back the gun and licked her lips to make the tingling go away. He was the devil's own. God, she was glad he'd come. Just this once. Even if she would never admit it out loud.

The past had slammed into her, knocking the breath out of her the moment she'd seen him. The power he had over her scared her spitless, so she'd gone on the offensive and attacked him. The only other choice she had was to collapse into his arms, and she couldn't do that. She couldn't give him a toehold. If she did, he would take everything and leave her empty again.

They were so close she could smell his tangy scent, feel his breath feather her cheek. She tucked her hands under her armpits so she wouldn't reach out to him in the darkness.

This was the man who took her virginity, ruined her career and broke her heart. In that order. Mike McNair was nothing if not thorough.

"Remember Captain Tchaikovsky?"

Of course she did. She grinned at the memory, glad it was dark and he couldn't see her. Captain Tassky had been one mean SOB, called Tchaikovsky because he was considered a regular nutcracker. He was also the man who had sent Mike and Tessa into the woods with nothing but a pup tent and one knife between them for a two-week survival exercise. Which was exactly what Mike wanted her to remember.

"I haven't thought about Special Forces in ages," she lied.

"I thought about you every day," he said in a quiet voice.

Damn it. Why did he have to be like that?

His uncanny ability to unsettle her without half trying drove her mad.

"Remember how it used to be?"

Right. Sex. That's what he was all about. "Not really," she lied again, hating that she had to. It should have been true. She should have forgotten it, him, long ago. There had been other men in her life, in her bed, whom she did barely remember, but she still recalled Mike's touch with sharp clarity.

No way were they going to discuss sex. "They won't all come after us. Maybe two. At least one will stay with the other three crates at the research vehicle. They'll be faster than us. It won't take them much to fix the other sled. We'll be slowed by the weight of the crate we got."

"How long do the dogs need to rest?"

They'd done a brief stint of Arctic training, but it hadn't involved dogs. In that, at least, he would have to defer to her. "An hour would be fine, we haven't come that far, but we can't go out there until visibility improves. I don't want to run them onto sharp ice or into a ravine or a creek."

She fell silent for a moment. "I hate leaving the other team behind."

"Why didn't you bring them?"

"We'll be lucky if we can feed the ones we've got. The rest are better off at the trailer. It's stocked for them."

"Makes sense." He looked up as the wind shook their cover. "Did I mention I spent last winter in Siberia?"

"Doing what? The Russian Army has exchange students now?"

"Not exactly."

Damn him. He'd been on some secret mission. *She* should have been going on secret missions instead of stuck in research for the past eight months. She hoped he had frozen his ass off. No, no, she wasn't going to think about him in terms of body parts. That would take her down the slippery slope as fast as an avalanche.

"We have a good sled and good dogs," he said. "We're dressed for the weather. While we're trapped here, we can get some rest, inventory our resources and figure out a plan."

Not bad. He had gotten in all three points under "eliminating fear and increasing your chances for survival" within two minutes flat: have confidence in your superior—which he apparently considered himself—have confidence in your equipment, focus on the task at hand. Captain Tchaikovsky would have been proud.

"We have the dogs, the sled, the furs and

some extra wood." She rapped on the crate. "Two good rifles."

"A good knife, waterproof matches and a small survivor kit," he added.

She went through the pockets of the parka she'd taken. Her left hand came out with a bottle, the right with a cell phone. "Check this out." She handed them to him, pulling back too fast when their fingers touched.

"Well now, what's the challenge in this? We're as good as out of here." The bottle cap squeaked as he unscrewed it, the air immediately filling with the smell of cheap booze.

"You still go out with the boys?"

"I lost touch for the most part. I'm not in the army anymore." He screwed the cap back on.

She'd figured that from his comment about Siberia. As friendly as things were between the U.S. and Russia now, they weren't doing sleepovers just yet. "CIA?" He used to talk about giving that a try back in the old days.

"For a while."

"And now?"

"Now I'm here."

Fine. "Are you going to make that call?"

He was some kind of special commando, while she was in the U.S.A.C.E., U.S. Army Corps of Engineers. Hands down he had to have better connections.

He was dialing already. "No signal." He closed the flap with a click.

"We can try again once the storm passes."

"You could debrief me in the meanwhile. What happened with those men?"

She closed her eyes. Oh, damn. She didn't want to think about that now. Guilt was eating at her still, and anger for letting them take her so easily. She took a deep breath as Mike waited. Might as well get it over with.

"They came in the middle of the night. Roger opened the door. They shot him right away." She swallowed. "I don't suppose they viewed me as much of a threat. They didn't look like they knew what the hell they were doing, so I convinced them I could help. Told them I was an Arctic survival expert."

"You always thought quick on your feet."

The small compliment, the acknowledgment of her abilities, felt ridiculously good. Especially since she'd been beating herself into the ground over what she had and hadn't done, for not being able to save Roger.

Mike was moving around, but she couldn't see what he was doing. Probably just settling in.

"Did they hurt you?" His fingers brushed against her bruised cheek, but withdrew almost immediately.

"I tried to get away and fell down the steps, banged my head against the side of the trailer. My feet were bound," she told him, hating to admit her failure.

He said nothing for a while, until she thought he might have fallen asleep.

"They were coming from the direction of the pipeline instead of going toward it," he spoke up suddenly. "But they still had the explosives. Doesn't make any sense."

"Pipeline? We weren't anywhere near the pipeline."

"Exactly." He paused. "I came across some classified information. Supposedly,

those men are in some radical environ-
mentalist group. A few miles of the
pipeline are shut down for repair. They
were looking to blow it up."

"Nothing was said about that. They
were definitely heading home. They
sounded pretty happy about their mission.
The only glitch was, the plane that was
supposed to pick them up went down in
the mountains in that storm five days ago."

"Odd. Lift up a corner of this cover for
a second, would you?"

She slid over and did so on the opposite
side from where the wind was blowing,
letting in some light. Mike already had his
knife in hand, going at the crate. She
propped the opening with a rifle and went
to help him. "TNT?"

"That's my best guess."

The wood protested loudly, but after a
few seconds the lid popped off. Mike
picked through layers of padding before
the smooth sheen of metal became visible.
His hands stilled.

She didn't have to have the symbol of
yellow triangles explained to her.

Far more disturbing than a pile of explosives, the crate they cradled between them housed a small nuclear warhead.

Chapter Two

"Something tells me those guys are not ticked-off environmentalists." Mike swore as he put the crate's lid back on. This changed everything.

Snow swirled into the tent, but he barely saw it. Did the CIA know about this? A number of things made perfect sense suddenly. Did the Colonel know?

"Weapons dealers?" Tessa went to check on Sasha.

Apparently satisfied with the dog's condition, she removed the propped rifle and let the cover drop, shrouding them in darkness once again, closing off the cold that had been pouring in.

"It's ours." He stared in the direction of the warhead, although he could no longer see the crate. "I'm guessing the American half of the group was selling it to the Russians, then the plane crashed and they got stuck here. How did they get to you?"

"Snowmobiles. They were just about out of gas."

"What I want to know is, where the hell did they get the warheads?"

The wind whistled down the plain, shaking their flimsy shelter, but enough snow had fallen to have buried the edges and keep them frozen in place. He bounced the furs on top to shake off accumulation, to avoid the "roof" collapsing on them. A few tears here and there in the stitching allowed for air. They wouldn't suffocate as long as they didn't let the snow completely bury them.

"Where did you get this old thing?" He ran his fingers over the coarse fur.

"From the Inupiat."

"Close by?"

"About fifty miles west. But they've already gone to their winter camp."

"What were you two still doing here?"

"We had a plane pick up scheduled

for…" She thought for a moment. "Yesterday. Since we were planning on flying out, we didn't have to worry about an early snowfall closing Black Horse Pass."

"As best as I can remember the map, the nearest town should be about a hundred miles south?"

"On the other side of the foothills. We couldn't take the sled."

"How are your dogs at hunting?"

"That's not what they were trained for, but I suppose once they get hungry enough their instincts will kick in."

"I can carry Sasha, maybe make her a travois." The dog should be able to walk some, the wound wasn't that bad, but there was no way she could keep up with the others over long distances.

"There's a permanent Inupiat village about sixty miles northwest. We can make it there on the sled and wait for the rescue team. They'll have an easier time finding that than spotting us among the snowdrifts or in the woods."

Sixty miles. A hell of a lot closer than the town to the south. Still. "I hate the thought of going farther north. Any polar bears around here?"

"They'd be closer to the coast. If we come across any surprises, we have good guns."

She sounded calm and confident, reminding him of the jams they had fought themselves out of together. And that, of course, reminded him of the steamy nights they'd spent in each other's arms.

"So what are the chances of us picking up where we left off?"

He heard her swallow.

"We left off with you drunk and a half-naked woman in your hotel room."

"Before that?"

"You mean when you got me kicked out of Special Forces training and destroyed my dreams?"

"I'm not going to apologize for saving your life."

She was too stubborn to admit that she would not have made it through the obstacle course in the Florida Everglades, but he remembered the day in crystal-clear detail. He could be stubborn, too. Was he not a Scotsman by blood? She had scared ten years off his life.

She'd been sick with fever and weak from bleeding, hanging on to life by a thread after she'd fought off an alligator. She'd lain half under the beast without moving when he'd found her, and he had thought for a moment that she was dead. Turned out she'd just been collecting her strength to push off the gator. She'd had a badly broken collarbone, her body covered in bruises and cuts, some of which looked infected.

The sight of her had made him forget the test, the only thought in his mind to get her to medical help, to get her to safety. At the end, he'd gotten a special commendation for saving a teammate, while she'd gotten the boot. She had failed the course and lost her chance with Special Forces. When she'd been released from the hospital four days later, still steamed at him, he had made things worse by being drunk.

She had left, and obviously *she* had moved on.

He sure as hell hadn't pictured *that* during the lonely nights he'd spent thinking about her. He'd pictured her waiting, regretting her rash actions. Mostly, he'd pictured their reunion in detail. It hadn't looked anything like this.

He had deluded himself into thinking their breakup was temporary, that she would come back or that, if she didn't, he would go after her and charm her back to him. But he'd barely been in the country in the past few years. The odd week here and there he'd spent tracking her down as she'd moved around, and by the time he'd found her, it was time to leave again, without a chance to actually contact her.

He had never for a moment figured that by the time they hooked up again, it would be too late.

"Listen, about the women… They were there for Shorty." And he'd trounced Shorty good afterward for his role in the breakup, before he realized it wasn't Shorty's fault. He had the right to whatever entertainment he chose. Mike was the stupid idiot who'd thought his worries for Tessa would be best drowned on the bottom of a whiskey bottle.

"I swear to God," he said. "We went out with the guys and I drank a little too much. I was worried about you. I went back to the room and passed out. I woke up five seconds before you came in. Shorty must have brought the girls back. Can you believe he's married now?" He tried to change the subject. "Caught in the net. Never thought I'd see that happen."

She didn't look amused.

"I'm telling you the truth. I've been telling you the truth from the beginning."

"I didn't believe you then, and I don't believe you now." The steel in her voice told him she had made up her mind a long time ago.

Frustration pumped up his volume. "That's your problem, babe. Maybe if you trusted me more we would have lasted."

HIS WORDS HUNG in the musky air of the tent. Tessa wrapped her arms around herself. This couldn't be real.

He couldn't be here. She was dreaming.

The pain she had gone through after she'd left Mike three years ago, the long months she'd spent miserable without him, on the verge of going back and forgiving everything against all reason—she couldn't have made it through all that for nothing. She couldn't go back there. She had enough need for self-preservation to save herself, didn't she?

"If the weather doesn't hold us up too long, we can be a third of the way to the village by tonight. Starting out at first light, we'll definitely make it by noon tomorrow, the latest," she said in a matter-of-fact voice, glad for the darkness that hid her face.

"That eager to get rid of me, huh?"

He didn't know the half of it. Because as much as she had convinced herself over the past couple of years that she was over him, his reappearance in her life made one thing Alaskan-air clear: she wasn't even close.

"We weren't good together then, we wouldn't be good together now. Nothing's changed."

The wind picked up and roared like a

grizzly bear. Winter was coming. The faster they were out of here, the better—for a multitude of reasons.

"How can you say that?" Anger laced his voice. "We were great together. You left me the first time everything didn't come off perfect."

The accusation hurt.

Everything about Mike McNair hurt. It wasn't right. Love shouldn't be this painful. And she wasn't even in love with him anymore; the part of her heart that had held him once had been beaten numb.

They sat in silence until the wind stopped outside. She pulled up a corner of their cover, struggling with the weight of the fallen snow. "Better get moving." She looked out, holding her breath against the biting cold that met her. It wasn't snowing anymore, the wind had pushed the clouds to the east. The sun was low on the horizon, as always this time of the year, even at noon. They had about two hours of daylight left—still enough time to make some progress before they hunkered down for the night.

She propped up the opening and moved over to the dogs. "How are you doing, Sasha?" She scratched behind the dog's ears and under her chin, smiling when Sasha licked her hands.

The rest of the huskies got up and came for their share. "All right Blackie. No need to be jealous."

She took a minute or two to make sure each got some attention. She would be requiring a lot from them, with no guarantee for their safety or even dinner when they stopped for the night.

"Ready?" She glanced at Mike, who was doing his best to bond with the few curious huskies that went to check him out.

She trudged outside into snow that was a foot higher—three feet on the wind side where it was piled up against their shelter in a snowdrift. The dogs followed her without having to be told, jumping in the freshly fallen snow that would make sledding difficult until it froze hard enough to go on top of it instead of having to struggle through the loose mess. Snowshoes would have worked better on something like this. But even if they had them, they couldn't leave the dogs and the crate behind.

She harnessed the huskies while Mike wrestled the fur cover from the snow and put it back on the sled. He made a bed from it for Sasha and put her in the middle. Sasha protested halfheartedly, wanting to jump off, but in the end, decided to obey his command.

"I'll walk for a while," he said.

"Haa!" She set the dogs into motion without getting on the back runners, giving them a break.

She ran alongside the sled, behind Mike. They couldn't keep it up for long, but every little bit counted. The easier they were on the dogs, the longer they would be able to pull. Now that Sasha was out, the rest had to compensate.

The silence was like a wall around them, a solid presence, broken by nothing but the sounds of the sled, their feet on the snow, their breath that came harsher as they went on. Alders and spruce covered the gently elevating hillsides to the south of them, open snowfields as flat as an ice rink ahead to the northwest, the way they were headed.

The beauty of the untouched landscape was overwhelming, humbling. It calmed her, helped her to center herself, to focus, the edginess of the close quarters of the shelter leaving her, her lungs filling with fresh air.

A wolf howled in the forest behind them, and the dogs picked up their heads. Blackie, the lead husky, pointed his nose to the sky and answered.

The snow came to the dogs' bellies, and they were struggling, their progress slow. They covered miles that way before the going got easier and she finally got up on the back runners. Mike squeezed on the sled next to Sasha, facing the dog team. She didn't realize that he was on the phone again until she heard him talking.

"Mike McDonald here. I'm ready to be picked up. I'm heading to an Inupiat village about two hundred miles northeast from where you dropped me off."

"Povongjuag," she said, and he repeated it. "Whatever the price, man. Name it." He listened for a while before swearing and closing the phone.

He turned to her with a dark expression. "The pilot who dropped me off can't pick us up. This whole area has been declared restricted airspace."

Considering the nuclear warheads, that didn't seem unreasonable. Except— "Aren't you working for whomever declared the restriction? Why wouldn't they send a chopper for you?"

He swore again. "I chartered a private plane."

"You're here without authorization, aren't you?" God, she was stupid for not having figured it out before. But there had been too much other stuff to think about. His being alone made sense now. She had expected more of a SWAT style rescue if anyone came for her, but being saved suddenly and seeing Mike of all people had thrown her for a loop and she'd forgotten to question the odd details.

"Authorization or not, they'll still come and get you if you ask for it."

"The Colonel is going to fry my ass for this one." He dialed again. "McNair."

He was silent for a long time, his face closed. Apparently, his colonel had a lot to say to him. Judging by his expression, none of it was good.

"I would appreciate some help on this one, Colonel." Another pause.

"There is one man I trust over there, an old buddy of mine. Tommy Cattaro. If you can get in touch with him—"

Another long silence.

"Yes, Colonel. Povongjuag. It's an Inupiat village. We should be there sometime tomorrow. I could use a secure phone. There are a couple of things I need to debrief you on."

He listened again. "No, Colonel."

"Yes, Colonel."

"That was not my intention, sir."

"Is there an official rescue team?" she asked when he hung up.

"Somewhere, I suppose. The CIA is handling the case."

"Is that where Shorty is now?" Tommy Cattaro, aka Shorty, wasn't on the top of her favorites list, but if he could get them out of here, she'd make nice with him.

"We went over from Special Forces together. We worked a few cases on the same team before I got recruited to—someplace else," he said. "Nobody but the agency is allowed in on this one. That's why I had to go AWOL from my own unit. What would you have wanted me to do? I couldn't sit around waiting for—"

"AWOL? Are you crazy?" She stared at him.

He looked her in the eye. "You know how you used to blame me for not making it into Special Forces?" He blinked. "Consider us even."

She had trouble digesting the information. He had put everything on the line for her. She didn't know what to do with that thought, where to fit that knowledge. If he still cared that much for her— No. She wasn't going down that road ever again.

"So where did you go AWOL from?" The best way to stop him from getting to her was to keep him on his toes about his own business.

"We're going to have to go around that." He pointed at the forest of alders and spruce in front of them that reached like a finger into the frozen landscape to the north.

He was ignoring her question. She'd pretty much expected him to do just that. There was nothing she could do to make the man talk, if he didn't want to.

"Gee!" She turned the dogs to the right when they were still a good fifty yards from the trees, taking advantage of both the flat terrain and the windbreak the woods provided.

Ten minutes passed, then half an hour. She was thirsty, but not enough to stop and melt snow. Night would fall soon; darkness came by 3:00 p.m. this time of the year. They would have to stop and make camp, anyway. Had the cloud cover not built back up, the snow would have reflected enough moonlight to go by, but that was not the case.

Mike pushed off his hood and turned his head to the sky.

She did the same and heard the helicopter, slowed the dogs, fired her gun and waited. Sound carried incredible distances in the silence of the snowfields. The rumbling of the chopper weakened. Damn. The rescue team was heading away from them. Then the sound picked up again. The helicopter came over the top of the trees in a couple of minutes.

Mike was already on his feet, waving.

The Apache—CIA logo on the side—lowered between them and the trees, the noise scaring the dogs. She brought the sled to a complete halt and got off, followed Mike who was already running forward. She would have to ask the pilot to turn off the rotors or she'd never get the huskies on.

The chopper hovered in place. Mike was slowing in front of her, held up his hand as if in warning. She knew how to approach a landing helicopter, for heaven's sake. The training they'd received together hadn't been that long ago. She ignored him.

Snow swirled around them as the chopper's blades stirred up the air. She put her head down and stopped, waiting for the bird to set down. The bullets that hit around her took her by surprise.

What on earth? She threw herself to the snow and looked around. Did the gun smugglers catch up? She glanced up, expecting to see the chopper covering them, but instead, the man she spotted in the open door was aiming at Mike.

Nobody else on the ground, but them. No smugglers. She scanned the area behind her. They were clearly the ones under attack from the CIA chopper.

It didn't make any sense. This was supposed to be the rescue team. Mike had called in their location.

He seemed to have recovered from his surprise before she did and was shooting back, making the bird pull up sharply and bank to the right. Then her training and instincts finally kicked in and she sprinted for the woods.

She stopped halfway there, hesitated, looked back to the dogs. She'd left her rifle on the sled. If she could get that and the huskies... Mike was running, too, twisting now and then to squeeze off another shot, jumping over piles of snow as he went.

"Come on!" he shouted as he passed her.

They were close to the woods, twenty yards, ten, there. They didn't stop for a while, spurred on by bullets hitting the trees behind them.

After a minute or two, the shooting stopped.

"We have to go back and get the dogs." She was breathing so hard, she had to bend over. Sitting in a research trailer month after month, doing nothing but data analysis, had softened her.

"They're not interested in the dogs. They made it plenty clear that they want us."

"What's going on?"

"Damned if I know." Mike ducked behind a boulder and leaned against it, making room for her. He pulled the phone from his pocket, but it rang before he could dial.

"We're under attack."

He listened and swore alternatively, then after a couple of minutes held the cell phone away from his ear and shook it, pushed some buttons, listened again, slammed it into the snow. "Battery is dead."

"Extreme cold will do that. What did you find out?"

"It's classified."

"Like hell it is." She wanted to shake him. "Tell that to someone whose ass is not getting shot up by our own government. I already saw the warhead, Mike."

"I don't know everything."

"Give me what you have."

He still had the gall to think about it before he finally nodded. "Apparently, a cache of warheads near where your research station was parked was broken into."

"There are no military installations anywhere around here. Roger and I have been through the area a hundred times." She tried to think of anything that looked even remotely suspicious, but there had been no manmade structures at all, just open snowfields.

"Underground bunkers most likely. Apparently the U.S. warheads were supposed to be destroyed under the disarmament agreement after the cold war, but they somehow *disappeared* from the list and were forgotten." His words were underscored with a thick tone of irony.

"How does that have anything to do with us?"

"Some gun dealer got wind of it, and a few warheads were stolen. The whole environmentalist-extremists slash Alaska-pipeline tale was a cover so the CIA could close the area for a massive manhunt."

She stared at him as understanding dawned on her. "It would look bad for the U.S. Government if it turned out we're hiding stockpiles of nuclear weapons that violate international agreements."

"Right."

"But why are they after us? You and I didn't steal anything."

"Looks like that's not how the CIA interpreted things. You left with the weapons dealers. At one point your research station was almost on top of the bunkers. And I'm here against orders. They figured out that we knew each other in the past."

Wait a minute— "Go back to the bunkers part."

"The Colonel said—"

"That's what the readings were about," she blurted, interrupting him.

"What readings?"

"We were doing all kinds of experiments, taking dozens of readings on air, dirt and melted snow every day. We would settle into a spot, work for a week or two. When we were done with our work, we would move fifty miles to the next observation point and start over." They drove the trailer on the tracks for the big moves, but for everyday stuff they used the sleds to get around. "Then all of a sudden, a couple of weeks ago an order came in to do a reading for radiation."

"Did you find anything?"

"Nothing out of the ordinary. Roger thought maybe they had some intel on nuclear testing in Russia and worried about the winds. We had very strong winds out of the west at the time. The strange thing was, we were told not to put the reading in the observation log, and that there was no need to repeat it again."

"So whoever is selling the warheads is in a high enough position to ask a favor of the U.S.A.C.E. He wanted to make sure there was no radiation leak before he sent his men in there."

"Somebody in the army?"

He shrugged.

"And the CIA suspects us. It's ridiculous. We can explain."

The expression on his face was hard, the thin set of his mouth making her uneasy. "We are not going to get a chance to make explanations, Tessa," he said. "I know the guy in charge of the operation, Brady Marshall. He's a cleanup expert if I've ever seen one. He's heavily into leaving no witnesses."

His brown eyes burned into hers as he shook his head.

"There's more," she said instead of asking.

He exhaled, his breath forming a small cloud in the frozen air. "We had some disagreements when I was working for the agency. He hates my guts. I came across information that implicated him in some serious stuff. I didn't blow the whistle, but—"

"But if he takes you out, he can stop worrying that someday you will."

He nodded. "Sorry."

"Sorry for what?"

"You might have been better off taking your chances with the smugglers and working your plan." He sounded miserable.

She took a deep breath.

"Okay, I'm only going to say this once, and first I want to emphasize how much I don't want you to try anything like this in the future." She held his gaze. "I'm glad that you came and got me."

He blinked. "What? Have I gone mad from exposure already? Am I hallucinating?"

She couldn't help cracking a smile as she punched him in the shoulder.

The sound of the chopper taking off reached them. It was coming closer. She stumbled and fell headfirst into snow when Mike shoved her under a large hemlock and dived after her.

"A small warning would have been nice." She cleaned the snow from her face as they lay side by side without moving.

The chopper hovered for a minute or two then began circling, and after a while they heard the noise of its motor fade into the distance.

"It might be better if we stay out of the open for now." He crawled out first.

She ignored the hand he extended to help her. "I'm not leaving the dogs," she said, and as soon as she was on her feet, she started back the way they had come.

"That's not what I meant." He followed.

She slowed when they were close enough to see the edge of the woods. An ambush could be waiting for them out there. She moved with care, expecting at any moment a hail of bullets. Mike was as vigilant as she, communicating with hand signals. They passed the last couple of yards in a crouch, creeping from tree to tree.

They shouldn't have bothered. The chopper had left no men behind. There was nothing in front of them at all—the crate, sled and dogs gone. A single flare stood stuck in the snow, bleeding red smoke toward the sky.

"They'll be coming back for us." Mike kicked it over and buried it. "We're not going to make it to the village over open land."

"They took my dogs," she said, stunned, fury filling her.

"They're not going to hurt the dogs. They only took them to make things harder for us." He put a hand on her shoulder, but she shook it off. He shrugged. "What do you know about this area?"

The bastards took her dogs. A couple of seconds passed before she could focus on Mike's question.

"There are a few families who live this far up. Trappers. Most of them go into the towns for winter. A couple of them stopped by the research station over the summer. These people cover ground like you wouldn't believe."

"We'll go over the hills then. We'll either run into someone or reach a town sooner or later."

"Let's go." Determination filled her, anger giving her strength.

They were in the Alaskan wilderness without shelter and supplies, winter quickly approaching; the CIA was on a search-and-destroy mission to round them up; and for all they knew, the gun dealers were still after them, too, wanting back the warhead.

Nobody could ever say life was boring with Mike McNair around.

WHEN HE CLOSED HIS EYES, he could see the gently swaying palm trees on the hillside in Belize, where he had put money down on a house. South America seemed like an excellent place to disappear to— great climate, plenty of English-speaking people, and yet far enough from anyone who might figure out his role in the weapons heist.

"The Boss," his codename for the mission, leaned back in his chair. The warheads had reached port. It wouldn't be long now before they crossed the Bering Strait and arrived at the next station before their final destination. Once the crates were in Siberia, he would breathe easier.

There had been some minor glitches along the way, but nothing they couldn't overcome. It would be no more than two or three days until delivery, and when Tsernyakov got his warheads, he would release payment.

Belize: sunshine and long-limbed women with soft, tanned skin, and the money to afford them. And why not? Hadn't he sacrificed enough to deserve that?

He would have to fake his death, though, before he left. It wouldn't do for the law, or his "business" partners, to come looking for him. A fire perhaps—a body wouldn't be too hard to arrange. Or he could go out on a boat and pretend to be washed overboard. He put his feet up on the edge of the hotel room table and went over the list of possibilities.

The wife would get his life insurance and was welcome to it. She could go nag someone else for all he cared. The kids, both from her first marriage, had barely tolerated him anyway. He was nothing but the man who held the wallet, someone to go to for new shoes and tuition for soccer camp.

He closed his eyes and pictured an azure-blue sky above, could almost feel the soft, warm breeze on his face. The house had a veranda overlooking the pool. There were people around the pool in his fantasy—he would have plenty of friends. A tall girl of about twenty came up the veranda stairs with a martini.

"You need company?" she asked, her full lips turning into a suggestive smile. Her long hair spilled down her naked back, a few strands escaping to the front to curl around magnificent breasts that were left exposed for his hungry gaze.

He nodded as he took the glass, watched her push his legs apart and get ready to satisfy him. He closed his eyes and let his head fall back.

Chapter Three

Crunch, swish, crunch, swish. He would have given just about anything for a pair of snowshoes. Mike ignored the cold slush that had gotten into his boots. His gaze strayed to the low ridge ahead of them. They had been walking toward it for hours, yet it still seemed the same distance away, their progress hampered by the difficult terrain. He glanced back at Tessa who kept up without complaint. She walked with her head down, focusing on where she put her feet.

They pushed on, searching for shelter, a suitable spot to sit out the night.

"Here," he said finally, just as the last of the grayish light slid off the sky.

They were in front of a "wall" created

by the root mass of a fallen tree. He cleared as much snow as he could out of the hollow the roots had left behind in the ground, and lined it with hemlock branches, the result looking like a giant dinosaur nest.

"Welcome to the Fresh Air Hotel." He grinned at Tessa, wanting to lighten the mood.

"What, you didn't reserve a room with a hot tub?" She was already picking up wood for their fire.

He went to help her. "The place is booked solid. We were lucky to get any room at all."

"Hmm." She gave him a fake grumble. "Remind me not to let you plan any more vacations for us in the future."

As hard as they tried, their jokingly spoken words didn't quite cover their unease. He was alert to the slightest noise around them, and from the way she stopped every few seconds to survey their surroundings, he knew Tessa was, as well. There were wolves out there. And possibly bears, too; winter had barely started. Nature had its own stragglers.

He dumped an armload of branches and went back for more.

Once they had enough wood, it didn't take much to get a good fire started. Although the kindling hadn't been as dry as he would have preferred, the alcohol acted as a decent accelerant. Their spot was sheltered from the wind, and they sat between the tree and the fire, the root wall behind them reflecting the heat back, so they were warm on both sides—as comfortable an arrangement as anyone could hope for under the circumstances.

He dumped the contents of his tin emergency kit at his feet, careful not to lose anything, then filled the tin with snow and melted it over the fire, giving Tessa the water. He melted another batch and drank next. They had to take turns, each getting a few swallows at a time.

After they rested a little, they collected more wood, enough to keep the fire going for the night.

"Wish we had that fur cover," she said, dislodging the snow that had caked on to the bottom of her boots.

He wished for a number of things, none of which he cared to share, pretty sure she wouldn't appreciate them. Instead he moved over to a tall pine and dug in the snow under it until he found a good handful of cones. Tessa helped him defrost them over the fire. They ate pine nuts, not enough to fill them, but sufficient so they wouldn't have to go to sleep with that gnawing feeling of hunger inside.

He sat cross-legged and patted his thigh. "Come over here. You can use me for a pillow. I'll take first watch."

They couldn't both sleep. Somebody had to stay awake to feed the fire. Without it, they'd be frozen by morning. And they needed it for reasons beyond heat, too. The flames would keep away predators.

She hesitated, but seemed to reach a decision at last and curled up next to him with her head on his thigh, facing the burning logs. "Wake me in a couple of hours."

He looked away from the silky red hair that spilled out of her hood and over him, feeling his pants shrink a size smaller.

Offering himself for her pillow seemed a less-than-brilliant idea now. He had thought only of her comfort, that he wanted her near. He hadn't thought it through to what the sight of her head in his lap would do to him. At least he didn't have to worry about falling asleep on his watch. He was way too uncomfortable to nod off.

A wolf howled deep in the woods, and another answered. He pulled his gun closer, ready for anything, the memories of his trek across the Siberian tundra rushing over him. For once he welcomed them, glad for a moment of distraction.

He had sworn he would never go near snow again as long as he lived. But then he'd found out about Tessa. He'd been alone in Siberia, but had his full pack with all the survival gear anyone could wish for. Right now, he had nothing but Tessa. All in all, a good trade. The fire lit her face, played on her long eyelashes. He put his left arm over her shoulder in a protective gesture, but she immediately shook it off.

"Keep your hands to yourself, buddy."

The woman was nothing if not stubborn.

"Come on now, lass. I dinna mean harm. Don't be scairt. I promise not to eat ye 'less things get real desperate," he said in his best highland brogue, trying to warm her to him by joking, but she didn't respond.

He'd let her get the bluster out of her system. She would come around.

Soon her breathing evened, and her face relaxed. She had to be as exhausted as he was. The cold took a lot out of a person, and they hadn't had enough to eat to replace the lost energy. He would try his best to shoot something tomorrow. He wasn't picky. A muskrat would do.

He reviewed their situation, planned for the upcoming days as best he could, while listening for any sounds of predators on the ground or choppers in the sky. The dark didn't mean they were safe from detection from above. Even if he kicked snow over their fire at the first sound of a helicopter, the CIA had plenty of night-vision equipment.

He woke her at midnight, to get his own

rest and because she would have had a fit in the morning if he hadn't.

She blinked slow and long, nodded. She didn't offer her lap as his pillow.

SUNLIGHT REACHED THEM at about ten in the morning, and even then they did not see the sun, only its gray reflection in the sky. They had been walking for hours by then, catching a lucky break with a bright moon and temporarily cloudless weather. They kept going, hungry, bundled up against the cold, hoping to find a road they could follow to civilization.

Mike shot a snowshoe rabbit a little after noon. They gutted and skinned the animal quickly, before it had a chance to freeze. Neither wanted to waste daylight, but they agreed on stopping long enough to make a fire and roast the meat.

The going was slow over the rough terrain, darkness coming too soon again. They'd been following a semifrozen creek. Tessa stepped out of the woods and stopped at the edge of a clearing, squinted her eyes. *Wait a minute—*

"Heard something?" Mike came up behind her.

She shook her head and pointed. "Over there." She moved toward what she had first taken for a giant snow-covered boulder. She could make out some evenly spaced logs, the slope of a low-pitched roof. She felt shaky for a moment, unsure whether from excitement or exhaustion.

"A cabin!" Mike fought his way toward the buried structure, pushing the snow aside.

He cleared a door by the time she caught up with him, grinning from ear to ear when he aimed the gun at the padlock. The shot echoed through the forest.

"I wonder how far that carried." She glanced at him with a twinge of unease.

He shrugged. "If the CIA is around, they are in a chopper. If they are close enough to hear a shot we'd be able to hear the rotors. I don't think they have a good enough location on us yet to send in a ground team."

"People live in these parts. Not everyone goes south for the winter."

"Good. If one of the neighbors comes over to investigate, he can help us figure out the fastest way to the nearest town."

He kicked the door in, and a good pile of snow went with it. She stepped forward first, peering into the darkness, moving to the right and staying still until her eyes got used to the dark.

The one-room cabin was small, ten by twelve maybe, with a sleeping loft above the general living area. There was wood stacked in the kitchen next to the iron stove, canned food on the open shelves. She went to light a lamp and turned it up, while Mike cleared the snow from the vinyl-covered plywood floor and closed and barred the door behind them.

He flashed her one of those sexy grins that used to get her every time. "Didn't I tell you we'd be fine?"

"If I recall correctly, you said you wouldn't eat me until all other options were exhausted." She was still not completely immune. She couldn't help grinning back.

"Well, we're not out of the woods yet."

He wiggled his dark eyebrows and snapped his teeth.

She threw her glove at him and gave him the iciest glower she could muster, not an easy task with heat spreading through her body at his lighthearted banter and the playful look in his eyes.

He caught the glove and stalked closer. "Let me at least take a look at what I won't be having. You have to take off those frozen clothes and get your circulation moving. I can help."

She'd just bet he could. Her body was squealing, "Yes, please!" Fortunately, she was smart enough to ignore it. She put the stove between them.

"It's not going to work." She couldn't count how many times he had charmed her like this, or when all else had failed, tackled her, bringing them both to the ground, tickling her until she let go of whatever she'd been mad about. "We need to start a fire," she added in a voice of measured reason.

He lifted his hands in capitulation. "I'll do the fire. Why don't you scare up something to eat?"

True to his words, he had a fire going by the time she wiped the frost off the cans, figured out what was what and opened two beef stews with a knife, since she couldn't find the can opener. She dumped the contents into an iron skillet and set it on the stove, stepping around him as he was trying to coax the small flames to grow.

God, it brought back the past, the two of them working together like this. She moved away to put a little distance between them, pushing back the memories that rushed her. They'd had some good times; she couldn't deny that. But had it been as special as her mind was now making it out to be? Was it only that he was her first real love, her first lover? That was it, she was sure. Every woman must have a special place in her heart for her first. She shouldn't make too much of the feelings that had risen from the past to confuse her. She made a point of turning her back to Mike and busied herself in the kitchen.

Within minutes it was warm enough to take her parka off, then her mukluks—the sealskin boots that had kept her feet warm and dry. She got up to stir the food but he beat her to it, so she sank back onto the overturned bucket she used for a seat.

He tasted the stew. "Almost."

He'd undressed, too. He looked good, even with his dark hair all mussed, or maybe especially because of that. It lent a boyish charm to the man whose towering height and wide shoulders would have been intimidating otherwise. His body had grown leaner since she'd last seen him. His impressive muscles were still there, but he had lost a lot of the roundness and softness. He looked harder, edgier, more dangerous—very much like one of those highland heroes on the covers of her mother's historical romances.

His cinnamon eyes locked with hers as he extended the wooden spoon toward her. "Want a taste?"

She pushed to her feet before she knew what she was doing and walked away. Not that she could go far. She reached the other side of the cabin in a half-dozen steps. "No," she said. "Thanks." She grabbed the notched ladder and climbed to the loft, the space so low she couldn't straighten.

She shouldn't be thinking about Mike now. She needed to think about how they could get out of Alaska.

Open shelves covered the walls around her, a large bed of furs in the middle. She should have brought the lamp. Pictures were tacked here and there to the shelves, of a family she could barely make out.

A large chest stood at the foot of the bed. She hesitated for a moment before opening it, then she was glad she did. She must have emitted some sound of triumph, because Mike called up to her.

"Find something interesting?"

"A CB radio." She was already hauling the thing out of the chest and bringing it back down.

"That's my girl." He closed the stove's door and came to her, cleared room on the table. "Put it over here. There must be an antenna on one of the trees."

They were saved. The tension went out of her all at once. When he lifted his hand for a high-five, she smacked hers into it, excited and filled with hope. They'd done it!

He turned the radio on. No sounds, no flashing lights. She reached for the volume button and twisted it all the way to the right. He flipped through the frequencies as they held their breath. Nothing.

The CB's battery was dead.

MIKE ATE TOO FAST, impatient for the stew to cool, and burned his tongue. Damn. Tessa shook her head as he sucked in air through his teeth. She stirred her meal, got a spoonful, blew on it for a while, then tasted it tentatively. Smart woman.

"Best stew I ever had." The corners of her mouth turned up before she swallowed the glob on her spoon whole.

He was about to crack a joke when the sound of a chopper came from above. It was moving on, not pausing above them as far as he could tell. Still, they couldn't stay here for long.

"We should leave in the morning," Tessa said, voicing his thoughts.

Her blue eyes seemed to dance in the

firelight that glinted off her reddish brown hair. Her curls tumbled to the middle of her back. He would have given anything to be able to run his fingers through them just now.

He used to joke that her red hair was a warning flag to alert the unwary to the fire she had inside. She might have been a small package—only came up to his chin—but she was no pushover. She was feisty as anything, bullheaded, but with a heart as big as the endless landscape that surrounded them—a heart that had once belonged to him.

Whatever it took, he would win it back again.

"I don't like the way you're looking at me," she said.

She was a suspicious one, but she would come around. He was sure of that.

"I was thinking about how to get out of here. I'll look for snowshoes, make some if we can't find any." He glanced at the open shelves in the kitchen, the row of canned meat. "There's enough food to take with us. We'll grab some extra furs, too."

She hesitated before she spoke. "What if snow already closed off the pass?"

"We'll come back here and winter over." If Brady's men from the CIA found them, they would deal with that when the time came. His escape and evasion skills had been honed by years of nearly impossible missions. And the Colonel would be asking questions about him if he didn't return soon.

"If I could get a message to the Colonel, he could pass it on to Shorty. Shorty would find a way to come and get us. He hates Brady as much as I do. Maybe more."

"Why?"

"Remember what I told you about Brady?"

"You had something on him."

"He was taking money from the budget. He requisitioned equipment that was never delivered. He fudged the inventory. We were risking our lives out there in the field, and the clips we had were short on bullets."

"And you found out but didn't do anything about it?"

"Couldn't. I went to him to tell him I knew what he was doing. Next thing I know, Shorty is begging me to leave the guy alone. Some chick in accounting made some accusations of sexual harassment. Shorty swore up and down he was innocent. He'd just gotten married. Brady offered to make the whole thing go away if I got off his back. He knew Shorty and I were friends. He promised to quit messing with inventory. There wasn't much I could do. I had little proof to start with."

"Hmmm." Tessa straightened her spine. "What's that?"

Wind howled outside, but he picked up something else, too, a rumbling kind of sound that came from close by, almost as if from inside the cabin.

"Probably the air, coming down the chimney," he said after a moment. Then he heard something else, something heavy moving on the other side of the door, and the growling became louder.

"Bear." The short hairs on his arms stood straight up. He glanced to the sole window, but it was covered with thick wood shutters outside.

"A grizzly," she said calmly and reached for the gun.

"Could be a black bear." Not that they were less dangerous, but at least they were smaller, easier to bring down.

She shook her head, turning as the logs rattled behind the stove. "We woke a grizzly. They don't truly hibernate, it's more like they go to sleep."

"The gunshot." When he'd shot the lock off, the sound had echoed in their small canyon.

"That and the smell of food."

The bear growled again and clawed on the logs outside, shaking loose some of the moss chinking that had kept the draft out. Its paws banged on the low roof. She was right. Definitely a grizzly. A black bear couldn't reach that high.

But the logs and the cabin held. Still, the bear spent a good half hour trying to get at them before it gave up and lumbered away.

Mike opened the door inch by inch. The bear tracks were a good reminder to be careful. The small clearing around the house was empty. Nothing charged from the woods, but he didn't feel confident enough just yet to walk all the way to the creek. He stepped away from the house far enough to fill a metal bucket with clean snow, then went back in, barring the door tightly behind him.

"Here, I'll do that." Tessa was no longer holding the gun. She took the bucket from him and set it on the stove.

Better make himself useful. He picked up the lamp and walked around, inventoried the contents of the cabin. The area under the sleeping loft seemed to be used mostly for storage. After he moved some boxes around, he found three pairs of snowshoes. He'd look them over and pick the two best later. Next to the door, half-hidden by a stack of metal cans, he came across a lidded plastic bucket.

"I think I found the bathroom."

She glanced in his direction and nodded. "The honeypot. That's what the trappers call it. I'm glad we won't have to go outside." She turned back to the stove. "Water is ready."

He eyed the ladder. "I'll check out the loft. Why don't you wash and do whatever you have to." He climbed up to give her some privacy, checked out the bed, dug through the chest, but found little that would have been of use to them. Then he looked up and found more storage, and a large green sack tucked onto a shelf.

"Got ourselves a tent," he called down, feeling more optimistic by the minute. He pushed back the bag and fingered the material inside: double-sided, a good four-season tent. Excellent.

He rummaged through the rest of the stuff until Tessa came up.

"Your turn."

He handed her the lamp, the eight-by-eight platform seeming to shrink to half its size now that they were sharing it.

"I'll be right back," he said, and climbed down, eager to slip under the covers next to her with as little delay as possible.

THE FIRST TIME she woke, it was to a sharp pain in her feet. They seemed to be freezing. They were freezing! The cabin was dark; no glow came from the stove below. Their fire had gone out.

She was pressed against Mike, snuggled into the nook below his chin, his arms around her. They were clearly on his side of the bed, so she couldn't even be mad at him for taking advantage. She had gone to him—for heat, nothing else. Her exhausted body had migrated toward the nearest heat source in the cold night.

She sat up and reached over him, trying to get the lamp without having to come out from under the covers. He came awake and alert instantly, seizing her, making her sprawl on top of him.

"Tess?" he murmured in a sleep heavy voice and pulled her up, rubbed his large hands down her arms. "You're cold."

They were face-to-face, just about every inch of their bodies touching.

"The fire is out. I'm going to start a new one." She lifted up to pull away.

He gathered her back to him. "Stay. I'll warm you."

He had tried to get her warm when they'd gone to bed, but she had resisted the temptation. She wasn't going to fall into the trap now. She was almost twenty-eight. Old enough to know better.

"Let go," she said in a voice that would have made the toughest drill sergeant proud.

"Why are you doing this to us?"

"There is no us." The sooner he accepted that the better. "You ended us three years ago."

"You walked out."

"You gave me some damned good reasons."

And there they were, at a stalemate again. She rolled off him.

"You stay here. I'll go." He grabbed the lamp and lit it, was on his feet before she could think of any good reasons why she should protest.

Let him go, if his macho ego needed to do it. He had to handle everything, never could accept that she was strong enough, never could take her for an equal. It was one of the things that had undermined their relationship, more so perhaps than that last night at the hotel when everything had blown up.

She snuggled into the covers that were

rapidly losing heat without him, relieved when ten minutes later he slipped back in. She made sure she stayed on her own side.

"Okay, I'll knock it off. I won't try anything. Come back here, at least until the fire gets going good. There's no sense in getting sick just to make a point."

She *was* freezing, curled up into a ball on her side. She inched closer, making sure to keep her back to him. She stopped as soon as she could feel his body heat, without actually touching.

"You have got to be the most stubborn woman." He grabbed her around the waist and pulled her closer, spooning her body with his. "Go to sleep."

He left his arm around her, and it felt so good she didn't have it in her to push him away.

The bear, she thought, forcing her mind to other things. They would have to be careful when they left the cabin. And the wildlife was only a small part of the danger that awaited them. She had a feeling that, come first light, the CIA chopper would be back.

THE NEXT TIME she woke, it was to the sounds of a motor, and she scrambled around for the rifle she couldn't find, registering that she was alone in bed. Her body clock said it was morning, but no light filtered in from outside.

"Mike?"

She looked over the edge of the loft and found the main room empty. The fire was burning hot in the stove. He'd been up for some time.

The sound of the motor wasn't coming from above. It came from outside the cabin. She made it down the ladder just as Mike walked in.

"I found a generator in the shed," he said with a huge grin on his freshly shaven face, dragging an electric cord behind him.

A small transformer and the radio were already set up on the table. He hooked up everything, looking as if he knew what he was doing.

He turned the dial, picked up the handset, switched through the channels until they heard someone talking. He rattled off some funky code name. "Mike

McDonald here. I'm up by Loggers Creek, does anybody have a copy?"

A few seconds passed before the staticky response reached them, the disembodied voice identifying himself with a string of numbers. "It's Jonah from Indian Valley. Are you up here trapping? Go ahead."

"Yeah. Not getting much, though. I ran into some trouble and I'm a couple of days late. You got access to a phone? Over."

"Sure. Need a message passed along? Go ahead."

"My old man is probably getting worried about me. Would you mind calling? You can call collect. Over."

"No trouble at all. Go ahead."

Mike dictated a number. "Tell him, I'm fine. I'm heading toward Black Horse Pass. Over."

"You need any help? Want me to call the ranger? You said you ran into trouble. Go ahead."

"Three hoodlums. We were checking on a friend's cabin and they came at us. Two Russians, one local. They took most of our supplies and busted up my boy pretty good. Watch out if you see them. Over."

"I will. Thanks for the warning. Go ahead."

"You know if the pass is still open? Over."

"It was two days ago when I was up that way. We haven't had much snow since. Go ahead."

Mike thanked the guy for his help and put down the handset. "Let's grab something to eat and move out."

They were packed and ready to go, Mike about to put away the radio when a message crackled through from Jonah.

"I was just talking to my brother-in-law in Nome, telling him about those criminals loose in the woods down here. He said four men, some ours, some Russkies, offered him a boatload of money to take them to Uelen with their crates. Go ahead."

Mike sat up straight. "Did he do it? Over."

"Weather is too bad up there. I told him to stay away from them. Go ahead."

Mike signed off and swore.

"Four? Sounds like the guy you shot at the edge of the woods made it," she said.

"That's the least of our problems. They're taking the warheads to Siberia."

She'd figured as much. Uelen was a small fishing town on the Russian side. "The CIA will catch them."

He shook his head. "The Colonel said they were focusing on the Canadian border. Maybe they didn't figure on anyone going north this time of the year. I bet they don't know the Russians are involved. They can't cross over into sovereign Russian territory, anyway."

He was right. That would cause a major international incident.

"And they can't ask the Russians for help, either. The warheads aren't supposed to exist." He shook his head.

"Those crates can't reach the black market. If they do—" She didn't even want to think about it. "We have to go after them."

He nodded, and the enormity of the task left her speechless for a moment. They had to make their way across the Alaskan ice fields, evade the CIA, follow a group of weapons dealers into Siberia and retrieve a couple of stolen nuclear warheads. All that with the Arctic winter snapping at their heels. She didn't want to think about how slim their chances of survival were, let alone the chances of success.

It didn't help that her partner was the one man she'd sworn never to trust again as long as she lived.

Chapter Four

They trudged through the grove of pines, heads down to protect their faces against the wind and the frozen specks of snow flying at them, some sharp enough to draw blood. Mike walked in the front, trying to block as much wind from Tessa as possible, frustrated with how little protection he could truly give her.

A shadow moved among the trees, just outside his range of vision.

A timber wolf.

It wasn't alone. The pack had been following them for almost an hour. This one was closer than the others had been, though. They were getting braver.

Mike picked up speed, walking with a purpose that showed strength and betrayed none of his exhaustion, relieved when Tessa pushed harder, too, and kept up with him. They could not afford to appear weak.

"How many?" she asked from behind.

He should have known she would notice. "A dozen. Maybe as much as twenty." The wolves would not yet come out into the open, but soon. They were getting impatient.

The winter light wasn't much, and the pines blocked most of it. He was hoping for a better place to fight them than this patch of woods. He had precious few bullets left, none that he could afford to waste.

The walking wasn't hard, the snow good and frozen, plenty of support for the snowshoes. They had to go around trees and bushes and boulders here and there, but that was all part of the terrain, part of what made this land beautiful. If not for the wind and the wolves, their passage could have been pleasant.

He glanced at a set of day-old tracks that converged with theirs.

"Snowshoe rabbit," Tessa said.

He looked around, and although he couldn't see a single wolf now, he sensed them. They were still there, stalking, hunting. He had hoped they would lose interest eventually, or get distracted by the scent of another prey. They had likely seen men before, were afraid of the gun, or they would have attacked already. He pushed on.

"We can't keep up this pace for long."

"I know," he said.

He was starting to sweat, too, the curse of any prolonged exertion when a person was wearing as much clothing as they were. He'd borrowed a parka from the cabin that was thicker and heavier than his own, wanting to blend in should someone spot them, trying to avoid being seen in something that was clearly military issue. This coat, unfortunately, was not made of special fibers that wicked moisture away from the body. Damp undergarments could kill a man in this weather as fast as any pack of wolves. They drew heat from the skin.

Mike strained his eyes to see ahead.

Soon they would have to stop, set a fire and get dry. But not yet. They were in a bad spot where they would be easily surrounded and attacked before the fire grew large enough to protect them.

His shoulders relaxed when he finally glimpsed a lighter spot through the trees ahead, some kind of open area, either a meadow or the end of the woods. They had to reach that.

A good twenty minutes passed before they finally made it, stopping at the edge of the open snowfield that stretched in front of them. He spotted a large brown shape a hundred yards ahead and squinted. It was a bull moose, his breath a frozen cloud in the air above him. The animal had pawed the snow off the ground in a windswept spot and was grazing on the frozen tundra grass.

Mike lifted his hand in warning for Tessa, but he didn't have to. She was already squatting in the cover of a leafless berry bush.

The wind blew from the direction of the moose. Good. Maybe it would give the wolves something else to think about.

He waited, shivering. They would have to start a fire soon. The predators would have smelled the bull by now. What were they waiting for?

He looked at the formidable double rack the animal sported. Perhaps the wolves thought their chances were better with the humans. Seemed a safe assumption on the face of things, two scrawny humans as opposed to a bull moose in his full power. He would just have to stack the odds in their own favor again.

The bull lifted his head and looked in their direction.

Mike lifted his rifle and took aim. The sound of the discharged weapon echoed through the plain, tearing the silence. The moose stood still for a moment then shuddered, but did not fall.

Did he miss? Mike glanced at the gun. The cold shouldn't have affected it. Not by that much as to miss a huge animal like that altogether.

He took aim again, just below the neck this time, between the shoulder bones, at the heart. But before he could pull the trigger, the animal collapsed in a heap, sending puffs of snow into the air.

Mike took a moment to gather an armload of fallen branches from around them then made a run for it. "Come on."

Tessa was right behind him. "We're going to need more than this." She dropped her load of wood and went to move the snow from around the animal without having to be told.

As soon as they had enough clean ground for the fire he started one, using the shelter of his body while Tessa built up a windbreak of snow. They worked well together, in harmony, without direction given or the next step discussed. They each knew what needed to be done.

"I'm going to get more wood." He left her with the safety of the flames, his rifle slung over his shoulder.

"Be careful," she said, not that she had to.

He crossed the short stretch of open land, but did not go into the woods. He skirted the tree line instead. Shadows moved impatiently not a dozen feet in. The smell of blood mixed with the smell of humans had to be tantalizing for the wolves.

He piled on as much wood as he could. They'd better have a large fire while they rested.

When he was done, he walked backward, not daring to turn his back on the sharp-toothed hunters. It would be too easy for them to sneak up quietly from behind. He hoped that if they did attack, he would have enough time to drop the wood and take good aim.

But the wolves waited patiently, perhaps for nightfall, perhaps because they were spooked by the smell of smoke.

"How do you feel about fresh meat?" Tessa smiled at him when he got back, and he forgot all about the predators.

She had already cut two double palm-size slices and laid them in the snow, tingeing the white with red.

"Some seasoning would be good," she said.

A flash from the past hit him. "Do you remember the rattlesnake stew?"

It had been the first time she'd told him she'd loved him. And it had scared him to death. He would have given anything now to have that moment back.

"I don't want to remember," she said slowly, as the smile faded off her face.

Funny how much pain a few little words could inflict. That was a surprise to him. The power of her words, that he could be hurt. He'd never been before, not by a woman.

He glanced over to the edge of the woods where the wolves waited, then started a separate fire and built it high for protection while he let the first one die down so they could use the hot embers for cooking.

Where had the pain come from? From vanity? He'd been rejected before, not many times, granted, but he'd never given those a second thought.

Before Tessa, no woman had been more than a game to him. Tessa, too, to be honest. She'd been the one woman among the trainees no man could get, no matter how hard he had tried. Mike had been cocky enough to find a challenge like that irresistible. That's how it had started. But something had changed. He could not forget about her like he had about the rest.

He would be smart not to push her. She was stubborn that way. If he pushed, he might push her away. And he wasn't sure what else he could do. He was a soldier, trained to fight to achieve his objective, to take it by whatever force necessary. And this was one situation where being aggressive would never work.

Frustration rose in him swiftly. "So what, you hate me now?"

She watched the fire, thinking, and it bothered him how long she took to think.

"I used to," she said at last in a low voice, lifting her gaze to his. "I cursed you a time or two while I was stuck in the research trailer for months on end." She shook her head.

"And now?"

"What happened, happened. You can't be anybody else but who you are." She fell silent for a moment then went on. "I'm sorry I socked you at the trailer. When I saw you, all that old stuff came right back."

"I'm not the same person anymore," he said, hoping desperately that it was true.

"Really?" She gave him a halfhearted grin. "Going AWOL on a madcap rescue mission that has as much chance of succeeding as a snowshoe rabbit against a grizzly in a fist fight... You're right, it's not as crazy as some of the stuff you've done. It's even crazier!"

He couldn't help grinning back. "I changed in *other* ways."

"I'm sure," she said more soberly now. "You're a good man, Mike. But I'm sorry, I can't love you again. Not anymore."

She skewered the meat on two sticks and damn if it didn't feel like she was skewering some vital organ of his. He had hurt her, badly, worse than he had ever imagined, he saw that now on her face and hated himself for it.

"So what were you and George working on?" he asked, having had about as much of the previous topic as he could handle. Not that he was eager to bring up the man who had "tried" to be her boyfriend.

"You know I can't tell you."

"Developing some new biological weapon for arctic warfare?"

She turned the meat. "Hardly. Small-time lab testing."

He took off his parka to let the clothes dry underneath, took their lunch from her so she could do the same and kicked off his boots. They sat in silence for a while, ate when the steaks were ready.

Moose meat was rich and dark, and they were both happy for it, a welcome change from the canned food they'd brought from the cabin.

Tessa picked up her head.

He looked toward the woods. The wolves were pacing around but keeping their distance. He scanned the sky as he heard the rotors of a chopper.

"Lie down."

She did so without a moment of hesitation, without asking questions, an instinct they'd both developed during their Special Forces training when their lives had often depended on each other.

He pulled the tent from its carrying case and covered her with it, shoved in her mukluks, her snowshoes. He pulled on his parka, and by the time the chopper came over the tree line, he looked like any lone native hunter, enjoying the spoils of his kill.

He was acutely aware of several things at once: the chopper's hesitation, the rifle within arm's reach, the distance to the woods. He looked up and offered a friendly wave. They were far enough away not to be able to see his face.

The helicopter circled once then moved on.

"You can come out," he said when it was safe.

"Do you think they recognized you?" She pushed back the tent canvas.

He shook his head. "I have a different parka on and I'm alone. They're looking for a man and a woman."

She folded up the tent and put it away. "We should go. We have less than three hours before nightfall."

He got up and warmed his hands by the fire one last time before sliding them back into his gloves. After she'd done the same, he kicked snow over the flames.

They moved out briskly. He carried the backpack while she handled the tent—and had gotten about a hundred feet before the wolf pack took over the kill. He turned back at the sound of snapping teeth and growling, the pack leader establishing order. Blood splashed onto the snow, innards dragged between two animals that were playing tug-of-war. "That should keep them for a while," he said as he turned back to walking.

"Hopefully by the time they get hungry again we'll have passed out of their territory." Tessa walked next to him, and even through the parka, he could see the shiver that ran through her body. Her face was set with determination, but he saw the aversion and twinge of fear in her eyes.

The wolves bothered her more than she let on. He would protect her with his life; she had to know that. But being the mule-headed queen of independence, Miss I-don't-need-anyone, she would bloody consider it an insult if he reminded her. Women were a troublesome bunch on the whole. It figured that he had to go and fall for the most stubborn of them all. Penance for his misguided youth and other multitude of sins, no doubt.

She picked up speed and he pushed harder to keep up. Wolves and helicopters aside, they still had over a hundred miles to go before they reached Nome and no time to waste in getting there.

THE WIND HOWLED, but they were comfortable enough inside the small tent, snow piled high outside for insulation. Amazing the difference a single candle could make in a well-made tent. Its light was a big improvement to sitting in the dark, and it gave just enough warmth to take the bite out of the cold.

Between the flickering flame and their own body heat, they were comfortable enough to sleep. Not that she could. Tessa turned her head and found Mike watching. His cinnamon eyes looked black in the semidarkness, the strong line of his jaw covered by rough stubble, a major weakness of hers. The soft prickle on her skin as he would tease her by rubbing his face over her neck, her inner thighs, her secret sensitive spots, used to drive her crazy. It was as if each hair connected with one of her nerve endings and sent electricity zinging through her body.

She looked away. All she needed was for him to pick up on her fantasizing about him. There'd be no living with the man.

"I'm sorry," he said, and she brought her head up sharply. "About everything."

Sorry? Mike McNair had made a virtue of never being sorry about anything. It was his main philosophy that life was meant to be lived instead of analyzed and felt guilty over.

He *had* changed after all.

"It's okay," she said, and took a deep breath. It was okay, wasn't it? They were teammates again, almost friends. They had a military objective, which they would have to achieve. They had to find a way to work together.

"Okay?" He raised a dark eyebrow and came up on his elbow.

The tent really was small. As hard as she tried, she couldn't keep their bodies from touching. She watched his head lower as if it was happening to somebody else. His lips, warm and soft, brushed over hers and left them tingling.

Not *that* okay, she wanted to say, but before she could, he leaned in and nuzzled the crook of her neck, gently scraping the beginning of his beard over the second most erogenous spot on her body. Heat and need flooded her in an instant, and she cursed him for knowing her so well yet shivered in delight as he kept up the small rubbing movements.

He did not fight fair, she thought in a haze as moisture gathered between her thighs. Every cell of her body remembered him and welcomed him back, singing the Hallelujah Chorus. He knew exactly what drove her crazy and he was merciless in his pursuit of her capitulation. He went for her weakness and exploited it to full measure.

A soft sound escaped her throat, and he had the gall to chuckle against her heated skin. Then he dragged his lips back to hers and took them fully this time.

A second of pleasure. It was no great sin, was it? Not when it might be the last they had with weapons smugglers waiting for them ahead and wolves and the CIA searching to take them down. Just one unreasonable moment of bliss. If there was a reason why she should deny herself that, it escaped her now.

She sank into the feel of him, floating on an invisible tide. If she had had any questions over the years whether the blinding heat between them had been just an exaggeration of her memory, she had her answer now. It was there, all there, in its full power as if not a day had passed since they'd lain in each other's arms exhausted from passion.

There had never been another man like him for her, and damn his hide, she was pretty sure there never would be again.

She drank in his familiar taste, his familiar scent coming home to her nostrils, invading her body as his presence was invading her thoughts and his tongue was doing its best to invade her own. She was sure that's what it was to him, too. No more—an invasion. Mike McNair liked to conquer. He'd had quite a reputation when she'd met him. And, like a fool, she'd believed that all had changed when they'd fallen in love. If he'd ever loved her at all.

The pain of it, the shame of her humiliation burned her eyes as she pushed him away. "No." She passed the single word through her sensitized lips.

"I'm sorry," he said again.

It irritated her to see that he truly was, and that he was as shaken by the kiss as she. She reached to gather the old anger, but it slipped from her fingers. "How long are we going to torture each other like this?"

"I don't know." He shook his head as if to shake off some spell. "I don't think I can let you go."

Irritation filled her again. She liked the feeling; it helped her resistance. "You had no trouble letting me go for the past three years."

Silence stretched between them.

"At the beginning, I was sure you would come back. I was mad at you for jumping to conclusions, hurt that you didn't trust me. I was too damn proud to go begging after someone when I hadn't done anything wrong."

She could see the truth of it in his eyes. Damn. Had she been so stupid?

"All the stories about you, I'd heard dozens like that." She offered her feeble excuse.

"Not after we met." He shook his head. "If you'd listened…"

No, she hadn't been in a receptive state. She'd gone to him to chew him out in the first place, to yell and rage at him for carrying her out of the swamp and ending her SF career before it started. The tramps at the hotel had pushed her over the edge. There was no coming back after that, no seeing reason.

She'd been one of five women, provisional trainees, allowed in the Special Forces training because of their outstanding record in the army. The gender-requirement policy set by Congress and the secretary of defense in 1994 excluded women from combat billets in the military. There were no women in SF nor were there any female SEALs.

After 9/11, however, it became clear that the country needed these special military groups more than ever. There had been some support for inclusion of women as a way to increase numbers, and a provisional program was started by Special Forces and kept quiet. It was little more than a test. There had been no promises for inclusion even if the five women allowed into training passed the rigorous requirements. The powers that be just wanted to know if it could be done.

It couldn't. One of the female recruits had gotten injured two months into training and had to drop out. Another left soon after, unable to stand up to the psychological strain. One got kicked out for fraternizing with a superior officer. One failed the explosives exam. Tessa had lasted the longest.

She hated to fail, and in this case it felt like she'd failed not only herself but her gender.

She'd been so stupid. She should never have trusted Mike. To carry on a clandestine relationship with him had been insane enough, considering that kind of thing was strictly forbidden. And with reason. When he'd seen her in the swamp he'd been too attached, too emotional. Two other trainees had gone by her by then. Both had understood that she did not want their help. Neither had forced it on her. Mike, however, had not taken no for an answer.

Failing the training half broke her. Walking in on Mike's betrayal in that hotel room, after she'd gotten out of the hospital, had finished the job.

He was watching her closely now. "If I could undo that day, I would, believe me. I hadn't realized what a big deal that was to you. To me it was a misunderstanding. I figured I would explain and we'd make jokes about Shorty's sexual appetites. I never for a moment thought you'd up and leave."

"You could have come after me," she said, unwilling to fully accept blame.

"I was sure you'd come back. I was an idiot. By the time I figured out you were gone for good, I was out of the country on a mission. When I came back, you were deployed."

"There were other things that didn't work between us. The drinking scared me, too."

He looked surprised for a moment, then the expression slid off his face. "Because of your father?"

She nodded.

"We weren't alcoholics for heaven's sake. We had some good times. We drank. That's what guys do when they're on leave. We were just a bunch of dumb-asses trying to outdo each other in whatever ways we could."

He was right. She knew he was. She didn't want to talk anymore about it, saw no sense in dredging up the past. She said nothing.

"How can you pretend it's over? You can't tell me you don't feel something. Some of what we had is still there."

Yes. Her body still hummed with the power of his kiss. "It's not enough," she said.

"I'm not giving up." Determination filled his eyes.

"Fair warning." She nodded. "But this time I'm not giving in."

He blew out the candle, and she could hear the sleeping bags rustle as he lay on his back. "You drive me crazy."

"See?" She seized on his words. "It shouldn't be like that. When a relationship is meant to be, it should be—" she searched for the right words.

"Nice and easy?"

"I'm pretty sure that's a hair-color brand." She rolled her eyes in the darkness. "But easier, yes."

"Why?" He wouldn't let it go. "What's wrong with difficult, as long as it's worth fighting for?"

"You can talk your way out of anything." She huffed, frustrated.

"It's just one of my many special skills," he said in a suggestive tone.

"And you never can stay serious long enough." But she couldn't help a smile.

God, she had missed him.

"How is Grandpa Fergus?"

He didn't respond at first. "Doing good now."

"Now?"

"He had some trouble with cancer, but

he beat it. We all knew he would. He's way too stubborn to admit defeat."

"Jeez, who does that remind me of?" she joked, but the news shook her, although she'd only met the old man once. He was a real character, that one.

Mike used to entertain her with his grandfather's outrageous highland tales during the endless hours of guard duty they'd pulled together.

Snow fell on the tent above them, the crystals frozen enough to make a sound.

They listened to that and the wind. Her mind ran through the past as Mike lay still next to her. He was probably mulling over whatever X-rated thoughts he usually entertained himself with at bedtime.

"My back is hanging out of the cover," he said after a while, justifying her suspicions.

"You just want to get closer."

"If I get sick, I'm not going to be much help to you. If you have no pity in your heart for me, at least consider the importance of our mission."

The man would not quit. Might as well

give him a snuggle if he was willing to be content with it. God knew, she had little resistance should he set his mind to something more.

"Come closer, then," she said.

He did, snug against her back, his heat immediately spreading through her body. "Brings back some memories, doesn't it?" he whispered near her ear, his hot breath playing with her hair.

A quick succession of pictures flashed into her mind of the last time they had made love. He'd made her want him until she'd lost all thought of caution. He'd been gentle and sweet, humming with barely restrained passion as he made sure she was ready, touching her body with awe and reverence that had turned her to mush inside.

"I prefer not to dwell on the past," she said, and ignored her body, which demanded a return trip to the happy place.

Heat spread between her thighs as she remembered him parting them, the way she'd caught her breath as he'd settled over her. They'd had to be quiet. There were men sleeping in tents all around them, two to a tent. She'd reached up to link her fingers together behind his head and pulled him down for a kiss. He swallowed her moan when he entered her. He'd been infuriatingly slow, careful not to shake the tent, not to make the slightest noise.

He'd been careful but thorough. He had made her his that night, in every way possible, and if she'd had an ounce of energy left, she would have begged for more. She hadn't realized back then just how dangerous that was, to give herself so fully, to open herself up to so much possible pain.

She cleared her mind. "I don't remember much. I haven't thought about us in a long time."

Mike ran a hand down her arm. "You know what they say. Those who can't remember history are bound to repeat it."

"There'll be no repeating of anything. Period." She willed her body to cool.

He put his arm around her and pulled her tight against him, ignoring her warning, always taking more than she was prepared to give.

"That hand better be in the exact same spot when I wake up in the morning." She had to draw the line somewhere, show him he wasn't fooling her one bit. "Move it an inch and lose it."

She couldn't let him know what a pushover she really was.

HIS MEN WERE three days behind. It made him nervous. The Boss switched his phone to voice mail, not wanting to listen to another scathing call from Tsernyakov. The man was not one to cross, nor were the Chechens, the final destination for the cargo.

He had to make sure to leave happy customers behind. He didn't need those kinds of people trying to track him down.

The delay wasn't his fault. He'd done what he could. He couldn't very well predict the plane crash. And there was no time to send in an extraction team. The alarm had been sounded by then, the area under extensive search. The best he could do was plant enough false information to make sure that the search centered on the stretch of land between the pipeline and the Canadian border.

Did Tsernyakov appreciate how risky that was? Did he thank him for sticking his neck out? Of course not. The bastard was frothing at the mouth, enraged about the delay, tossing around threats like snowballs.

The Boss kicked off his shoes and lay back on the bed, crossed an arm over his eyes.

He had other things to worry about besides being late—the witnesses. Two! The thought filled him with cold fear alternating with anger. He had hoped Alaska or the CIA would take care of them. He'd made sure they were considered suspects, had made a damned good case, but couldn't push beyond that. Not without raising suspicions.

He had missed his chance to take them out at the edge of the woods, cursed himself for that mistake still. There was no telling what his men had discussed in front of the woman, and whatever she knew she'd probably told McNair. Being the smart-ass he was, who knew what McNair had put together by now.

Damn. He let out his breath, willing himself to sleep, too wired to actually do it. Why the hell did McNair have to get involved? Never did know when to stay the hell out of everybody else's business. This was the second time the man had come close to ruining one of his deals. The first time he'd let the guy live. Big mistake. This time he wouldn't be so generous.

He opened his eyes and glanced at the clock on the nightstand. Tsernyakov was expecting a status report in another four hours. The bastard was a control freak, on the dangerous side of pushy.

The Boss closed his eyes again, wishing the whole thing to be over. He'd brought enough to the table, earned his fee. He'd been the one to know the location of the warheads, the one with necessary contacts to defeat security. But he couldn't use his influence to do more. Anything else that had to be done, he had to do on his own. There must be no more links leading to him.

He didn't think of it as murder. He'd killed before, for the good of his country. He could certainly do it again, now that his own future hung in the balance.

Chapter Five

The farther north they got, the sparser the
vegetation became, the trees shorter and
shorter, offering less and less protection
against the Arctic winds. They had seen no
sign of the wolves or any other wildlife for
some time.

"Chopper," Mike called out, and they
jumped at the same time, threw themselves under the nearest scraggly bush,
and scooped snow over their bodies.

The chopper came low. The short trees
allowed it as close as twenty feet.

"Don't move," he said, and closed his
eyes against the snow that the rotor blades
stirred up.

The icy crystals burned his cheek. Now
that he wasn't moving and generating

heat, his body cooled quickly. The parka and his sweater were wet around his neck, where some of the snow had gotten in and melted. He opened his eyes to a slit and glanced over at Tessa to make sure she was okay. She lay still, facing away from him.

The chopper hovered above. Could the men see their tracks? Mike swore under his breath. They'd been careful to disturb the snow as little as possible while they'd walked, moving along the natural curve of snowdrifts where their shadow would cover the snowshoe prints. The wind was blowing, too. Not enough to cover the tracks completely, but enough to soften them, to smudge them so they wouldn't stand out.

A minute passed, and another, then the chopper banked to the right and disappeared over the trees.

"They're not giving up, are they?" Tessa stood and shook off the snow. "I wonder if they got the other warheads."

"I'm thinking, no." He straightened the backpack he'd borrowed from the cabin, then fixed his left snowshoe, which had gone askew. "They must have expanded the search area. The last I talked to the Colonel, the CIA was searching way east of here."

He followed Tessa's gaze toward the north where the sky was already darkening—too early. It was barely past noon.

She glanced back at him. "Maybe it will pass us."

He hoped it would. Because from the looks of it, what headed toward them was a hell of a storm. Damn. They didn't need another delay. "Let's cover some ground."

She didn't have to be told twice.

They pushed forward at a good clip, neither of them caring now about getting sweaty. They had to go as far as they could before the storm hit. These Arctic blizzards could rage on for days.

He focused on nothing but placing his feet onto the snow at the best angle for speed, scanning their surroundings for shelter, something that would block the wind from the tent. The trees were thin and sparse, alders mostly, not much in the way of a windbreak.

The first squall reached them before they got half a mile. It whipped the existing snow around for a while, then the clouds opened and added fresh material.

They'd passed boulders the size of houses all through the morning, but nothing now, of course, not when they needed it. Damn, the wind was getting strong. They had gone on too long.

"The tent." Tessa had to shout even though she was next to him. The storm whipped the words from her lips, so he could barely hear. She dropped the carrying case to the ground and struggled with it.

He helped to loosen the string, threw himself on the billowing material of the tent as the wind ripped it from his hands and almost took it away. He stood on it with one foot while clearing snow with the other. The frozen ground was a few inches down. He worked up a good sweat by the time he beat the first stake in with a rock Tessa had found for him.

Once all the stakes were in, they set up the fly, despite how difficult it was under the conditions. It domed the tent, helping to better deflect the wind.

"Get in." He pushed her through the opening and practically fell in after her, zipped the door tight. He felt better adding their bodyweight to the tent and not relying solely on the stakes. With the ground being as hard as it was, he hadn't gotten them as deep as he'd wanted.

Damn, it was cold. The storm had brought the icy air of the Arctic.

He opened the backpack and tossed one of the sleeping bags to Tessa. Despite the cold, they were much better off inside their shelter than outside. Here, at least, they didn't have to contend with the windchill factor. The sides of the tent moved around, struggling to take flight. He rummaged around for the candle, then stopped. No sense lighting one until the wind died down, it would just be knocked over or blown out.

For once, she didn't have to be told to cozy up to him. He sat on his sleeping bag with his legs spread and she sat between them, her back pressed against his chest, dragging her sleeping bag over them for cover.

"Was it this bad in Siberia?"

Worse, he nearly said, before changing his mind. "No."

In Siberia, his life had been the only one in danger. This mission had higher stakes. He hated to see Tessa in jeopardy. He would have faced any hardship as long as he knew she was somewhere safe.

"I hate sitting around," she said, and he grinned in the dark.

She wasn't the patient kind. He couldn't blame her; he was the same.

"The storm is coming from the north," he said. "I doubt any ships will be leaving port in this weather."

She didn't respond.

"I'm worried about the dogs," she said after a while.

He pulled away to take off his parka now that they'd warmed up a little. They couldn't sit here fully clothed. They needed an extra layer when the storm stopped and they had to leave the tent.

"It's not in their best interest to abuse the animals."

She shrugged off the sleeping bag they used for a blanket, and took off her own coat. "They don't need them in Nome." She pulled the cover back on.

"They'll probably sell them or trade them for supplies."

"Or abandon them on the side of the road." Her voice held a fair dose of concern. "They might want to make as little contact with the locals as possible. They wouldn't want to be remembered."

"Like an abandoned dog team sitting for days in front of the general store wouldn't draw attention? People would remember who rode the sled in."

"You're right." She took a deep breath.

"I bet we'll see those dogs in a couple of days."

"I hope so."

He squeezed her shoulders. "We might not make it out of here alive, there's a load of nuclear weapons headed out of the country for who knows what purpose, and your biggest worry is the dogs?" He was just teasing. Actually her big heart was one of the things he admired most about her, the way she thought of and went to battle for just about anyone.

"We got ourselves into this mess. The huskies didn't ask for any of this."

"When we find them and take care of the smugglers, we'll adopt the dogs. How about that?"

She didn't respond, but he felt her shoulders relax against him.

The wind whistled outside, the frozen snow hitting the tent from the side making the pattering sound of raindrops. They were stuck here for a while—nothing he could do to advance their military mission. Might as well start pushing for his other objective. It was time he started to get Tessa thinking about the possibility of being with him in the future.

"I bet those puppies would be just fine someplace like upstate New York. God knows, the place gets enough snow." He ought to know. He'd spent more than one Christmas break there with his grandparents. "Ever thought about where you'd settle down if you got the urge?"

She stayed silent.

The main thing was not to get discouraged. She had allowed him that kiss the day before. More than allowed. For a few moments she had responded, the glimpse of her old passion blowing him away. He had every reason to be optimistic.

He nuzzled her cheek. He had a couple of ideas on what they could do for a little extra heat.

She turned her head from him.

"You know, you're a hard woman to forget," he said with an effort. It didn't come easy for him to admit even the slightest weakness.

"I'm sure you gave it your best try." Her voice was as cold as the air around them.

"I did," he admitted, and when she pulled away, he added, "I never could succeed, though."

He reached out and drew her back into his arms, turned her head so he could brush his lips against hers. She didn't pull away, but neither did she respond, not even when he shifted her until they were face-to-face and tasted her more fully, deepening the kiss.

She tasted so good. He wanted to taste her everywhere, promised himself he would, no matter how stubborn she was. He was plenty hardheaded himself, and single-minded, too, when it came to achieving his aim. He would not rest until he broke through the last of her defenses and made her admit that she needed this as much as he did.

He found the zipper on her parka in the dark and pulled it down enough to sneak one hand in. His bare skin soaked up her heat as he moved forward, mad for the feel of her, to glide his fingers over the body he wanted more than anything to belong to him. He cupped her heavy breast and groaned into her mouth, pushing her back to the ground, blinding need flooding his body until he forgot the storm around them, everything but Tessa in his arms again.

His muscles tightened, hardened. Almost there. He grabbed for the zipper on her pants. He'd waited a long time for this, too long. He had planned on taking it slow. Who had he been kidding? He couldn't, not the first time. It wouldn't matter. She had to be as ready as he was. She had never minded mindless, flesh-pounding passion. He remembered well how she used to meet him thrust for thrust.

His heart sang, his body just about burst with lust. He could think of nothing but sinking into her softness, having her slim legs wrapped around his waist as he drove himself home, plunged into her over and over again, made her forget the past three years, made her unequivocally, forever his.

He dragged his lips from hers to travel her face, to cover with kisses what he could not see in the dark.

Her cheek tasted wet and salty.

It sobered him in an instant, the wave of lust riding his body screeching to a painful halt. "Tess?"

He reached up to her face, his fingertips confirming the tears. Hell, he'd seen her in just about every state, but he had never seen Tessa Nielsen cry. It scared him as nothing else could.

"Tess?" He sat up and pulled her with him. "What's wrong? Talk to me, honey."

The mad desire in his belly turned to concern. What was wrong with her?

"You broke my heart," she said in a hoarse whisper.

The pain in her voice slammed into him like a battering ram.

He'd broken her heart.

"I'm sorry," he said, unable to come up with anything else.

Cold air wedged between them when she pushed him away. He reached after her but then let his hands drop.

He'd broken her heart.

And here he'd been thinking all he had to do was to fool around with her a little, seduce her some, tell her how much he had missed her, remind her of the good old times. He hadn't, not until this moment, realized how much he had hurt her, or considered that he might have hurt her beyond what could be undone. It scared the soul out of him.

"Are you okay?"

"Fine." Her voice sounded steadier now.

"I'm sorry." God, it seemed that was all he could say lately, and it was woefully inadequate. "I'll quit it," he said with sudden determination. "I mean, you don't have to worry about me. I'm not going to push you anymore. I've been a jackass."

She didn't say anything to that.

"I'm not gonna touch you ever again, if you don't want me to." He heard the catch in his own voice. "Just let's get through this, okay?"

"I'm a big girl. You don't have to worry about me." The irritation in her voice switched on his own.

He felt mad at no one in particular, bereft, bewildered. "Fine."

"Fine," she snapped back.

"Man, I feel like I'm in kindergarten," he said, disgusted with himself.

"Are you calling me childish?" That cold tone had returned.

He wished they could see each other's faces. "I was calling myself immature."

"That's the first thing we've agreed on in a long time."

He was frustrated enough to want to

pound something. It occurred to him that she might feel the same, that it might help her to get all that anger out. "Would it help if you hit me?"

A second of silence passed. "If it did, I sure as hell wouldn't need your permission."

Sounded like she was working herself up to a good righteous anger, part of it probably because she was embarrassed at having been caught crying. She took great pride in being as tough as nails. Losing it had to shake her as much as it shook him.

The best course of action seemed to be to keep his mouth shut. Why was it that he could be as smooth as the Arctic ice with any number of women, but when it came to Tessa, he could never quite find the right words to say?

He had broken her heart.

He had the mad urge to punch his own lights out.

Mike closed his eyes, willing himself to relax. They were safe, no one would hunt them in this weather, be it the four-legged enemy or the two-legged kind. He wasn't tired, but he hoped he could sleep. He needed the unconsciousness of dreams, needed his mind to be away from this tent, from Tessa, from the realization that he might have lost her forever.

THE STORM RAGED well into the evening, burying all but the very top of their tent. Getting out proved to be a tricky and messy business, snow pouring in as soon as Mike unzipped the entrance. It was like digging out from under an avalanche. But the necessity of team work at least broke the uncomfortable silence between them, even if all the conversation they had was "hold here," "hang on," "push harder" and the like.

"We should walk through the night," Tessa said. "We need to make up for lost time."

He finished packing his backpack and nodded. The sky was clear, the endless stretch of freshly fallen snow reflecting the full moon, so there was almost as much light as during the day.

He moved forward, following in her tracks, hating the awkward silence that settled back between them. He had promised to leave her alone, but this didn't seem right, either. If he were here with one of the guys from the SDDU, they would talk about old operations they had pulled together. That wouldn't work with Tessa. Clearly, she didn't want to be reminded of their shared past. With the guys, the topic would invariably end up being about women—yet another bad idea for this situation.

He kept his mouth shut.

The freshly fallen snow made for hard walking, regardless of the snowshoes. Instead of gliding on top, they kept sinking in. There were more obstacles in their way than before; the strong wind had knocked over a couple of scrawny trees, piled snow high in spots while clearing the ground in others.

One wrong step could land a person waist-deep in the snow, so they both paid attention to where they stepped. At least the land was flat, and he knew it wouldn't be long before they reached the end of the forest and were out on the open ice. The going would be faster, for sure, but they would also be easier to spot from above. He pushed the thought away. There was no sense in worrying about something he couldn't change.

The only sounds were the crunching snow beneath them and their breathing. She was tiring; he could tell from her uneven stride. There was no wind to block, so he let her lead, let her set the pace. A boulder blocked their path and she slowed but made no attempt to go around it. Snow had piled high on both sides. It would be an easy matter to go right over.

She went up, slid down on the other side. He followed. Then all of a sudden the earth moved beneath him.

A deep roar rumbled through the silence, as he tried to keep his balance, his arms flailing. He was being lifted up.

The second roar came, much louder than the first. The white snow beneath him rolled to the side and gave way to brown shaggy fur. God help him. He slipped and for a moment found himself sitting on the shoulders of a very large grizzly, right before the animal twisted, and he finally rolled to the ground.

The bear saw him, turned and swiped him with an enormous paw that sent him flying through the air, hitting the snow with a thud. His head swam for a moment, then his vision cleared and he saw the growling grizzly, moving toward him with its giant teeth bared.

Where was the rifle?

He searched the snow, desperate, calculating how fast the animal would reach him. It was in no rush, still shaking off sleep, confident in its ability to take care of one rude human.

Where was the damn rifle? He spotted it at last, the very tip of the barrel sticking out from the snow—too far away. He went for the knife in his boot, not a weapon to make much of a difference, but if luck was with him he could buy Tessa enough time to get away.

He tossed his glove, wanting to feel the handle in his bare palm, needing as good a grip as he could get. All right. Here came the beast with lumbering steps, shifting its weight now to its hind legs to better tower over him.

He didn't look at the face and the fearsome teeth now. He was watching the muscles, waiting for them to bunch, calculating when the animal would lunge at him. He needed all the leverage he could get. He came up into a crouch just as a snowball passed by the grizzly's head and smacked into his parka, in the middle of his chest.

What the hell?

"Over here!" Tessa screamed from somewhere behind the animal, and her next missile was aimed better, hitting the beast's ear.

It didn't even pause.

The next thing to come flying their way was a branch, then a pair of boots in quick succession, one right after the other, each hitting the bear in the back of the head. The animal turned with an enraged growl.

Mike swore.

As if just now realizing the trouble she was in, Tessa took off running over the snow, her snowshoes strapped to her sock-covered feet. She was no match for the grizzly who was over the fallen tree and in full pursuit within seconds.

Snow flew up as its giant paws smacked down, its massive body shaking the ground.

Mike lunged for the weapon. There. He cleaned the snow off and aimed. His fingers were trembling for the first time ever—not from the cold. He willed them to still, looked through the crosshairs.

No, not the heart. With an animal as huge as this, even with a hole in its heart the muscles would keep on moving for seconds, long enough for the beast to reach its prey. A head shot was difficult from behind. There was no more than ten feet now between the grizzly and Tessa.

Mike closed one eye, his heart stopping midrhythm as he aimed for the hump behind the bear's head. He squeezed off a shot, didn't dare to take a quick second for fear that the bear would jerk aside from the force of the first and he would hit Tessa.

He watched, his mouth dry, as the grizzly slammed into the ground, its spinal cord severed. It was dead, but its momentum carried it, and it slid forward with dagger-sharp claws stretched toward its intended victim.

Mike leaped forward. Too late, too late. God, he'd never moved faster in his life. But he was late. He saw Tessa go down. How bad was she hurt? He was almost there, then vaulted right over the bear to get to her, a roar of desperation caught in his throat.

She was sitting in the snow, looking stunned, two giant paws on either side of her, the snowshoe on her right foot literally in the bear's open mouth.

He took a moment to swear good and proper as he gasped for air, bracing his hands on his knees.

"What the hell were you thinking?" he yelled at her the next second, then gathered her into his arms and squeezed her until she made some sound. Then he remembered his promise not to manhandle her again and set her aside.

"Don't you ever do that again." The blood was slowly returning to his head.

He sank down where he was, on the

grizzly's head, couldn't find the strength to move to a better spot. His hands started to shake again, then his whole body. "Why in hell would you do something like that?"

She seemed to gather herself and gave him a thin smile, but her face was still as white as the snow at her feet. "I knew you would save me. You never could help yourself." The smile widened into a grin.

"Are you laughing at me?"

She nodded with mirth. "I've never seen you this shook up. That bear really scared you, didn't it?"

She didn't have a clue. "Yeah," he said. "The bear scared me."

Like hell it did. The sight of her in harm's way was what had cut him off at the knees.

She was still grinning.

He buried his head into his hands and groaned. Somebody had to either shake or kiss some sense into her. He couldn't have done the job even if he had the strength for it. He had sworn he wouldn't touch her.

"Has to be at least eight feet tall, if not taller." She measured up the bear.

He glanced behind him. It was definitely that big. And she'd gone up against it with snowballs and mukluks.

For him.

To save his life.

Something squeezed his heart; a funny fluttering feeling spread through his stomach.

"Thank you," he said.

"Same here." Her expression turned serious. "Good shot."

"Lucky shot." He'd been so scared for her it was a miracle he'd been able to see straight.

"Do you think it was the same bear that attacked the cabin?"

He got up and looked at the beast. There was no way to tell, they hadn't seen that one.

"Could be, they roam pretty large territories. Could be it was following us and got ahead of us in the storm."

"As much as I didn't like being stalked by wolves, the idea of being stalked by a grizzly sounds even worse. I'm glad you took it out." She was looking straight into his eyes.

"Me, too," he said, and, thinking of

the alternative, felt his knees go weak all over again.

She skirted the bear and walked back.

"Where are you going?" He wasn't ready to let her out of sight just yet.

"Getting my boots."

He got up and followed her. His backpack was somewhere back there, too. It had fallen off when he'd rolled off the bear.

"Now your feet will be wet," he said, looking at her snow-covered socks.

"At least I still have feet." She shrugged, and he felt a flash of anger that she didn't take the danger she'd been in seriously enough.

"We'll start a fire."

His insides were still shaking.

His next step took him directly into a giant paw print in the snow. His boot filled only about half of it.

She had followed his gaze. "I can't believe we killed a grizzly. This is turning out to be one kick-ass adventure." Her eyes sparkled, and he could practically see her swimming in adrenaline.

"Do you know how many hours I spent

daydreaming about missions like this while I was stuck in that stinking trailer?" She grinned.

He gathered some wood and thought of the crazy missions he'd been on, daydreaming about Tessa. Funny that while she'd been wishing for more action and danger, he'd been wishing for her, the only action on his mind in connection with her being X-rated.

She was driving him crazy.

He got the fire going, using the bear as a windbreak, and made her sit long enough to get dry. When they were done, he threw on his backpack and moved out, Tessa walking next to him.

She was going on about the bear and all the other exciting stuff she was going to get to do once they caught up with the bad guys.

He blocked her out. If all went well, they'd be in Nome by morning. And then he would lock her into the first hotel room he could find while he went and took care of business alone.

"Don't even think about trying to leave me behind in Nome," she said.

Scary how well she knew him.

She still didn't get it, though. "I want you safe because I care."

Her sky-blue eyes went wide for a second, before they hardened. "Obviously not enough. If you cared about me, you would care about what I wanted. You never understood." Her shoulders slumped as she turned away.

He really did want the best for her. But then why did he feel like such a jerk? She was right; he didn't understand. He had never understood. That was how he had managed to break her heart. "Explain it to me then."

She turned to him with a look of surprise on her face. Surprise that he was willing to listen? Hell, had he been that big of an ass?

"For one, I don't want to be anyone's little fragile woman, tucked under some man's wings." She took a deep breath and paused, waiting for his rebuttal.

He decided to do the smart thing for once in his life and just listen.

They left the last of the short twiggy

trees and bushes and reached the barren ice fields at last. Man, it was cold.

"I want to be able to trust the man in my life," she went on cautiously. "And I want him to trust me. Not just trust me not to cheat or something like that, but trust me to take care of myself, trust me to back him up when needed."

"I do," he said, and he meant it. "But to let you step into the way of harm— It goes against everything I am."

"I'm not one of your little sisters."

"Don't I know it." He shook his head. Truth be told, his three sisters had grown up while he wasn't looking and resented his efforts to protect them, with as much vehemence as Tessa did. They especially hated his talks with the boyfriends when he was in town. Not that he tried to intimidate the guys or anything.

"It's the way I was raised. Do you know how many times my grandfather told me that a Scotsman's biggest responsibility in life was protecting and loving his woman, giving his life if needed for his family?"

A smile hovered over her full lips.

"Yeah, you're a regular laird of the mist. Wanna step out of it and enter this century?"

He didn't. Not really. Right about now he would have been perfectly happy living in a less-civilized time when nuclear weapons hadn't yet existed, somewhere he could throw her over his shoulder, take her back to his castle, and that would be the end of that.

And for a moment he could see clearly—the two of them in an ancient tower room making love on a blanket of shaggy wolf pelts in front of the fire. He could have sworn he felt the heat of the flames.

He shook his head and picked up speed, his snowshoes gliding forward with ease. She had him tied up in so many knots, he was hallucinating.

MIKE WALKED, squinting against the bitter wind. All the canned food from the cabin was gone, no trees anywhere near and no chance of a fire. Tessa was struggling with each step now. He hoped they wouldn't have to spend another night on the snowfields.

They plodded on in silence as night fell, the stars coming out one after the other.

His eyes caught something in the distance, making him look harder. He grabbed Tessa's arm and pointed.

"What is it?"

"Lights."

"Nome?"

"Not yet," he said. "But probably one of the outlying villages."

"Let's go then." She picked up speed. "I'm ready to face the bastards."

Chapter Six

"Feeling better?"

Tessa blinked her eyes open as Mike came into the room with an armload of shopping bags. A moment passed before she remembered that they were in Nome's Lost Nugget, a quaint bed and breakfast on the edge of the small Arctic town that its inhabitants insisted on calling a city.

"I can't believe I fell asleep." She sat up and ran her fingers through her hair, blinked the sleep from her eyes. The short nap did little to remedy her exhaustion. All it did was make it clear she needed more sleep, lots more.

The aroma of food wafted through the door—probably lunch being prepared downstairs. Her stomach growled.

Mike dumped his loot next to her, looking at her with those swirling cinnamon eyes that were now filled with heat as they slid from her face to her bare shoulder. Then he shuttered his expression and stepped back. "Did you make it into the shower before you passed out?"

She pulled her shirt back into place and shook her head. She'd sat down to undress. That was the last thing she remembered.

"Want to do it now?"

"You go first," she said. He'd just come in from the cold, while she'd been snoozing under the blankets. He needed warming up more than she did.

"Okay." He grabbed a bag, then closed the bathroom door behind him.

The fact that he didn't crack a joke about not being selfish and invite her to share the bath was beyond weird and completely out of character. Then again, he had treated her with nothing but professionalism since her embarrassing breakdown and the following bear attack. This was what she wanted, wasn't it?

Maybe not exactly this. The old Mike

had gotten on her nerves from time to time, but the new Mike plain freaked her out. His behavior was…unnatural, confusing, irritating. Even more so because she wouldn't have admitted to missing the old Mike if her life depended on it.

She scooted closer to the bags and rifled through them—a change of clothes for her and a small first-aid kit. Then she found the source of the mouthwatering smell that filled the room and forgot about the rest of the stuff as she ripped the takeout containers open.

Barbecue ribs and French fries, a smaller container filled to the brim with a generous slice of apple pie, everything still hot. She stared at the bounty, regretting some of the uncharitable thoughts she'd been entertaining about Mike over the last few days. He had remembered her favorite foods.

The meat melted off the bones, the ribs cooked to perfection. She shoved a few French fries into her mouth, scarfing them down, realizing all of a sudden how truly starved she'd been. Relief flooded her as the food hit her stomach.

They had made it to Nome.

Over the last couple of days of snow-storms and other misadventures, she hadn't been always sure. But they were here in the city and they were alive and unharmed, save her feet, which needed some attention, not quite used to this much walking.

She was licking clean the plastic container that had contained the apple pie when Mike emerged from the bathroom. His dark hair was still wet, glistening in the light, his face clean shaven. He wore gray thermal underwear that covered him from ankle to wrist. *Snug* was the operative word. Tessa glanced away, then back. Little of his body was left to the imagination. Not that she had to imagine it. It had always been there in its wonderful, muscled glory, living permanently in her memory.

"Thanks for dinner," she said, and looked down at the empty containers, suddenly embarrassed. "It was for me, right?"

"I don't eat French fries," he said with disdain.

And that was true. Mike was more into health food when he had the choice, not that he wouldn't eat any number of disgusting things when he was forced to it. The rattlesnake stew came to mind.

"How did you pay for all this?"

"Western Union." He grinned. "You've gotta love them."

"You've made contact."

He nodded. "More than one. The Colonel put me in touch with Shorty. He's down by Fairbanks, working on this case. He'll try to get over here by tomorrow morning. I filled him in. He promised to give me as much help as he can. If he can swindle a chopper for a couple of hours, he'll provide me with backup."

And just like that, all the fuzzy gratitude over the ribs was gone in a moment, replaced by swift anger and a sense of betrayal. "*You* are going to have backup?"

"I thought you should stay here. I'll arrange for a transport for you. The Colonel is going to help you with the CIA. I explained everything to him. He is not going to let them get you caught up in some kind of witch hunt. Shorty is going to throw his weight behind us, too, although that might just anger Brady more. They can't stand each other."

She could tell from his face just how pleased he was with his arrangements. "Michael Fergus McNair—" she came to her feet "—I've been sitting in a godforsaken trailer for the past eight months, taking readings. If you think you can cut me out of the action now, you have another think coming."

She picked up a bag and threw it at him. It felt so good, she threw another.

"Easy now." Mike ducked. "I've been worried you might react like this."

"But you don't give a rat's ass, do you? You and your me-macho-man-must-protect-little-woman attitude."

The third bag hit the bathroom door an inch to the left of his head. And with that she was out of ammunition.

"As I was saying—" An infuriating little smirk played at the corner of his lips. "I was worried you might not take to that idea, which is why I asked for approval for you to join the mission, considering the likely case that you would follow me, anyway."

Her mouth hung open. Had he really done that?

He made a show of carefully picking up the bags and their spilled contents and putting everything on the table.

"Did I get it?" She held her breath.

"I'm sorry. Did you get what?" He looked distracted as if he'd already forgotten what they were talking about.

She threw a pillow at him. "Did I get permission?"

"Oh, that." He started to shake his head as he picked up the pillow, but then a huge grin burst across his face. "You did."

She wanted to jump on the bed like a five-year-old. "Thank you," she said as dignified as she could, regretting her earlier outburst. She grabbed the clothes that were meant for her and walked by a foolishly grinning Mike with her head up. She closed the bathroom door behind her, then locked it, needing to be in separate airspace if she was to keep from throwing herself into his arms.

She was in, officially in, on the action.

"I found out about the smugglers, too." Mike's booming voice came through the door right next to her, startling her into moving away.

"Did we miss them by much?"

"Just barely. They had some rough weather up here, too. The men and the crates shipped out this morning."

"How soon can we follow them?"

"At daybreak tomorrow. Two boats are headed out for Uelen, one Russian, one American. Well, the Russian for sure. The American captain is still thinking about it. There's a lot of ice in the strait. They're saying in a normal year shipping would be closed by now. It's only because of the mild weather they've been having that the harbor is still open."

"Will Shorty be here by morning?"

"No," he said. "But he knows to follow."

She stripped out of her clothes, glad to be done with the garments she'd worn for the past week without change. The bathroom was still steamed up from Mike's shower, soothing and comfortable. Hot water came at once, and she stood under it soaking up the heat as her muscles relaxed.

She was going on a top-secret commando mission. She grinned. This was what she'd wanted to do all her life. She was going to be so damned good, they'd never want to let her go.

Tessa lathered shampoo into her hair and rode a wave of blissful optimism.

By the time she was done, Mike was lying onthe middle of the bed, palms under his head, eyes closed. He still wasn't dressed, the thermal suit stretched over his muscles. Lord, but he had a fine body. At that moment she wanted it so badly it bordered on the pitiful.

"Are we staying in?" She would have felt much more comfortable if they went out scouting the harbor and the town, anything really that got them away from the intimacy of the small room and that bed.

"Until nightfall. The place is crawling with CIA."

"Do you think they know the smugglers were here?"

"Hard to say. They might just be covering

all their bases. Looks like their search had been extended to the whole of the state."

"Do you think they know we're here?"

"Unlikely."

She looked at the small, uncomfortable-looking armchair in the corner. "Are you going to sleep in the bed?"

"Unless you object." He opened his eyes. "Yer a bonny lass, but I'm a mite too tired for mischief just now," he said in the Scottish brogue of his grandfather.

His eyes were red-rimmed with exhaustion. He was worn-out by their trek through the wilderness, and so was she. The hot water had relaxed her muscles and they were begging for the bed.

Who was she kidding? Her body was begging for Mike's—especially when he talked like that—but, unlikely to get him, it was willing to settle for the bed.

"Fine." She sat on the edge of the mattress, and he scooted over giving her more than sufficient room.

She stayed as far from him as possible without falling off.

"Now who doesn't have any trust?" he

remarked dryly, and the bed shifted as he came up on his elbows. "Come to think of it, for someone who demands unconditional trust, you are awful stingy with it."

She was not. She turned to set him straight, but he cut her off before she could say anything.

"You don't trust me to know when you need help and to give it."

Was he right? Even as she asked herself the question, she knew he was. "It's dangerous to trust someone. What if they let you down?" God knew, she'd been let down before.

"What if they won't? You don't have to be strong every second. It's great that you are, but wouldn't you feel better knowing that someone was there to catch you if you fell?"

She wanted to believe that. But she couldn't. "I never had anyone I could trust that much in my life."

"Of course you had. At least your family."

Especially not her family. She shook her head as old memories crept in and heat stole into her face. "Just drop it."

"Tessa?" His face turned serious, his gaze searching hers.

"I don't want to talk about it." She hadn't, not once, to anyone.

He reached out to cup her hand that lay on the cover between them, but she pulled away.

"You can tell me anything."

Not this. It was too embarrassing. "It's not a big deal." Her father had told her so. She felt like such a wuss and a big sissy for still feeling hurt over it after all these years. "It's nothing." She had to let it go.

"The hell it is if it puts that look in your eyes." His voice came hard and clipped.

Oh, hell, she couldn't tell him, now that he'd made such a huge issue of it. He would think she was nuts for letting something so small bother her. He would probably laugh.

"You wouldn't understand."

"Don't cut me down like that. However colossal an ass I've been in the past, I do care about you. I always have, from the beginning, you have to believe that."

She felt something loosen inside her as she nodded.

"It happened a million years ago." She took a deep breath. "I was twelve." She fell silent. She couldn't do it.

A few seconds passed.

"Oh, man." His face darkened, and she could see in his eyes a hesitation that maybe he didn't want to hear this story after all. But then he reached out and took her hand again, and this time she didn't pull away.

"My father lost his job and couldn't get another. My mother tried to get some work, but she was always a stay-at-home mom, so people said she didn't have any skills. We were so poor, Mike." Their meals consisted of macaroni and cheese, spaghetti with sauce that had never seen meat, hotdogs wrapped in stale bread.

Then things got even worse when her father's unemployment ran out. "He drank a lot, especially in the evenings. Then even more when Greg died."

"Operation Desert Storm." He squeezed her hand, and she felt touched that he remembered.

She nodded. "Then my father's old boss came over one night and talked to my dad about going into business together. He'd gotten laid off, too, finally, but he'd gotten severance because he'd been a manager. It was enough to start something, and he knew my father was a work horse."

God, even her mother had come out of her stupor of grief for a while. She'd smiled for the first time in months.

"They started a landscaping business. Mr. Soniak bought the equipment, my father provided the facilities. Mr. Soniak lived in a condo in Pittsburgh. We lived on a farmette with a bunch of outbuildings. He knew the fancy neighborhoods where people paid big bucks for making sure their lawns looked as spotless as their neighbors'."

The business had taken off almost immediately. She could hold up her head in school again; kids no longer teased her about never bringing lunch and wearing clothes that were too small.

"The equipment was housed over at our place, so Mr. Soniak spent a lot of time there. He was single, probably bored at home, my mother used to say. I loved watching him and my father work on the machines.

"Sometimes he got back from his list of houses before my father did and he waited for him in the barn, oiling up the mower, filling the tank for the next day. My mother would send out a cold beer or a snack."

She closed her eyes, not wanting to go on. Why the hell had she started? Would Mike, like her father, tell her she'd been imagining things?

"Trust me," he said, and she nodded.

"He would pat me on the head sometimes, then on the shoulder. One day I was sitting next to him and he patted my thigh and left his hand there. I was too young. I didn't think anything of it."

She watched a muscle tick in Mike's face, focused on that.

"It was May and I was invited to a pool party at a friend's house. Mr. Soniak was in the barn. My father wasn't home yet. My mother was finishing dinner. She gave me a beer to take out to the man before I left. I was in nothing but a bikini."

Had it been as much her fault as anyone else's? If she hadn't run around half-naked, if she hadn't sat to stay awhile when he'd asked her.

"It was hot, too hot for that early in the year. He told me how much I'd grown and offered me a sip of cold beer, and I took it."

Maybe if she hadn't taken the drink, if she hadn't wanted to look older and so-phisticated in front of the man who was half her father's age and so full of charm and amusing stories, the man who was the very salvation of her family.

"I had a bottle of suntan lotion with me." That and a towel. "He told me he would put it on for me before I left."

Mike's hand tightened on hers.

"It felt funny having his hands on me. My mother put suntan lotion on me some-times, but it didn't feel like that. He took too long. He sat me on his lap and I squirmed."

That was it. She really couldn't say more now. Tears burned her throat, constricting it to the size of a needle.

A hoarse sound escaped from Mike and brought her gaze to his. "Did he rape you?" He was holding his breath for her answer.

"No," she forced out the word. "But he put his fingers inside my bikini. He hurt me," she said, wanting him to hear all of it now. "It was nothing. My father said it was nothing. He didn't take my clothes down and he didn't rape me. My father said I must have misunderstood an innocent gesture." The last words came out in a whoosh, rushing to reach the end of her embarrassing confession.

There. She'd said it now. She lifted her gaze to Mike's face, expecting to see confusion and the question "That's it?" in his eyes.

But his face was tight and dark as he swore and gathered her to him, held her in an embrace that was so infinitely gentle, it took her breath away.

"It was nothing," she said, echoing her father's words.

"It was everything," he said in a voice that allowed no argument. "He took your innocence. Your father should have killed the bastard."

"Our family depended on him."

"It shouldn't have mattered."

And to her mortification, she felt tears roll down her face. "My mother understood. She made sure I was never alone with Mr. Soniak after that."

"But she didn't call the police?"

She shook her head. "She would never contradict my father. It just wasn't her way. He supported us. He made the decisions. My mother would have been lost without him."

He swore again. "No wonder you don't trust anyone." He pulled back and brushed his lips over her forehead.

"I want to." She wiped her eyes with the back of her hands. "God, I'm such a sissy."

"You're as tough as nails. You're so tough, sometimes it scares me."

It was strange to hear those words come out of his mouth. She wouldn't have thought anything scared Mike McNair. She relaxed into his warmth and inhaled his scent, and when her eyes fluttered closed she fell into a deep dreamless sleep unlike the nightmares of helicopters and ill-mannered grizzlies that had plagued her short nap earlier.

HE KNEW WHERE THEY WERE. Being able to use the CIA's resources was a thing of beauty. Once he knew the warheads were out of the country, he had made sure the search switched its focus to the northeast. Every suspicious movement was reported back by the agents in the field, and he had access to the reports.

The Boss took his first easy breath in days. Everything would be fine now. Nobody else had enough knowledge of his various activities to finger him but those two, if they put things together... He couldn't afford to let that happen.

People in Alaska went missing all the time. Nobody would make much of it. The weather, as ruthless as it was, had a way of surprising unprepared tourists. The bodies wouldn't be found until the spring thaw. Unless, of course, the wildlife found them first, in which case the bodies would never be recovered at all.

This one last task he had to see to the end, then he would be on his way to Belize.

He let his eyes drift closed. Belize. There was a party by the pool. The young woman coming up to the veranda swayed her hips seductively, the sun caressing her breasts as he would caress them soon. He reached an arm out and she came to him with a smile.

THE CIA WAS THERE all right, not glaringly obvious, but not quite blending in, either. Tessa pulled her fur-trimmed hood deeper over her face as she passed a rental car parked in front of a shoe store, the man behind the wheel talking with lips that barely moved. If she wasn't specifically looking, she would have thought him a tourist, as no doubt many of the locals did.

The sky at 6:00 p.m. was as dark as in the middle of the night. She made her way toward the harbor without hurrying but walking as if with a purpose, blending in with the few people outside who were coming from or going to work.

She kept an eye out for her dogs and

spotted two huskies peeking out of the back of a pickup. They weren't hers.

A lot of the boats were already put up for the winter. It wouldn't be long until the harbor closed altogether, waiting for spring breakup. Looked as if it was under construction now. She eyed the giant seawall of granite boulders she assumed were there to protect the city, then she saw the two shipping vessels Mike had told her about and walked toward them. The dock was a short one, reaching into the sea no farther than an eighth of a mile. She wondered if in the summer months, when there was more boat traffic, ships had to wait their turn to come in.

To her credit she didn't jump when Mike suddenly stepped out of the shadow made by a giant pile of crates right next to her. They'd decided to come separately, taking different routes, being able to survey a larger area that way.

"Any trouble getting here?" He appeared relaxed, but she knew from experience that he was alert to the smallest detail around them.

"No." They fell in step. "I saw two possible agents. Can't be sure."

Another car sat at the end of the harbor. She could make out one person behind the wheel.

"That's another one." Mike confirmed without looking that way. "Walk slow. We won't be able to come back this way again without drawing notice."

So they had one chance to survey the two boats and decide which one to trust their lives to tomorrow—if the American captain decided to go, thereby giving them a choice. They'd better make note of everything. She skimmed her gaze over them. Both vessels waited in the back of the harbor, near the car. They wouldn't get a chance to stop and gawk for long.

"Which one is the Russian?"

"The smaller one," he said. "It got caught on the water in that storm two days ago and sustained too much damage to reach home port. They had to pull in here for repairs."

They were almost at the boats, their pace slowing to a stroll. Mike reached out his hand in a tentative gesture. She took it. A couple seeking a romantic moment by the water might appear less suspicious.

The boats were right in front of them, the surveillance vehicle not fifty feet ahead. They needed time, a few more minutes for a careful look. She stopped and took Mike's other hand, as well, turned her face to his, moving so her back was toward the boats and he had a perfect view. She knew nothing about ships; Mike would have to be the one to make a determination.

A cold breeze came off the dark waters behind her. It would be a perilous journey, her first time on a ship. She squeezed Mike's hand to help keep her doubts at bay. She glanced toward the car. The man behind the steering wheel was watching.

"Look like I'm saying something romantic," she said.

His gaze flickered from the boat to her as he pulled her a little closer and gave her a few moments of undivided attention. "I'm out of practice with romance," he said.

She gave an impolite snort. That would

be the day, when Mike McNair couldn't get a different woman every day of the week. Then the petty jealousy slipped away as she thought back to when they were still together, the nights they had spent under the stars, how little they had needed for happiness back then.

"Help me out. In another time, another couple— What would she say?" He interrupted her thoughts.

His breath fanned her face, ridiculously warm, visible in the cold air, tangible like a touch.

"I missed you." She swallowed. "A woman might say that."

His gaze hesitated on her face before slipping to the boats behind her. "He missed her, too. I'm sure he would tell her." He waited a beat. "What else?"

The stars above them seemed to shine with new brilliance.

"If they had fought before, she might tell him she's sorry."

"Does she still care for him?" He pulled her into a full embrace, but kept his attention on the task at hand.

"Maybe she's scared to." Her heartbeat doubled.

His parka was soft, but she could feel the hardness of his body beneath it, the steel core that drew her and scared her alternatively. He was a strong man, the strongest she knew. Could she ever keep her own strength, stay independent next to him, when leaning on him seemed so natural? Would she lose herself if she gave herself to him? And if she lost herself and he let her down, what then?

"I'm thinking he does. Care for her." He focused on a point behind her, the familiar line of his jaw covered with the beginnings of a stubble. "No need to apologize for the past then."

"Maybe he's sorry, too?" she whispered.

"More than words could say," he said.

"Sometimes people fight about stupid things."

A car door opened, then closed. Neither of them looked in the direction of the sound, but both were acutely aware of the shuffling footsteps coming their way.

"Does she love him?" He was looking at

her now, his eyes swirling pools of darkness, their intensity freezing the words in her throat.

"I don't know. Maybe. Maybe she's fighting it," she said at last, her voice rusty. Were they still talking about some imaginary couple?

The man coming toward them was no more than twenty feet away.

Mike dipped his head, but stopped short of touching her. She wanted the reassurance of his lips. She wanted him to claim her, to make things easy for both of them. She couldn't keep up this tug-of-war anymore. Did it really matter who won?

He hovered, watching her. He wouldn't kiss her, she realized, and disappointment slammed into her at the thought. He would keep his promise not to push.

The footsteps slowed as they neared.

She stood on her tiptoes and pressed her lips to his, watched as his eyelids slid closed, his thick, dark lashes trembling. The first touch was a shock, sweet and blinding like the opening of heaven's doors.

He didn't move, but waited for her to do

as little or as much as she pleased. She brushed her lips across his warmer ones, a slow pass then back again. A tentative nibble on his lower lip sent her blood rushing. Then he opened to her and she promptly forgot that all this was only for pretend.

She could never get enough of the taste of him.

They had kissed a hundred times before, a thousand, but never had it been like this. He didn't try to arouse her, distract her, placate her or comfort her with this kiss. He was simply there, having given up all his power for her to do with him as she pleased.

Oh, he responded, and she felt the hunger under the iron control, but he made no move to get the upper hand, no attempt to master and to lead. It left her more breathless, more completely lost to him than if he had.

She explored him anew, learning him, sinking into his familiar places. It seemed they had been apart for a thousand years, or none at all, any thought of further separation all but unimaginable.

His mouth was soft and warm under hers, supplicant.

A challenge rose from inside her after a while. She mastered him because he let her. This was no true victory. The goal became then to snap that steel will, to take his control, to make him lose himself to her passion.

She tasted him, teased him, nibbled, bit hard, then stroked gently with her tongue. She was tearing down his defenses, could feel them crumble. Trouble was, her own were coming down, as well. As he was losing himself to her, she was losing herself to him.

She felt his hands fumble with the opening of her parka and arched against him, urging him faster, waiting for his hands to find her feverish body. But the caresses didn't come.

She pulled away after a few moments to look at him, confused.

He was holding the fur trim that lined the zipper, his hands white-knuckled and trembling. Then she looked up, into his eyes, and saw the effort it took, the panic that he couldn't hold much longer, the desperation of wanting to keep his word to her.

She felt childish all of a sudden, embarrassed. She leaned her forehead against his throat, her body weak with need.

"I'm sorry. I shouldn't have," she said when she straightened and pulled away.

He flashed her a look that asked who she was kidding, then took a deep breath and looked around, reminding her why they were here in the first place.

The man was back in his car. He had likely walked to the other end of the harbor and back, passing by them twice without her noticing. Her embarrassment kicked up a notch.

"Look," he said, and turned her gently.

The sky lightened over the sea, as if a painter had dragged his brush across black canvas, leaving a mesmerizing swirl of pale color behind.

"The aurora borealis," she whispered.

The purplish pink magic grew as it ribboned through the sky. As many times as she'd seen the northern lights, its foreign beauty never ceased to fill her with wonder.

She felt Mike's solid strength behind her and leaned back into it, her face turned upward. "Breathtaking, isn't it?"

"More than that," he said.

They stayed until the wind coming from the water picked up and chased them away. The man in the car watched them closely as they walked by him. She kept her gaze on Mike and didn't have to pretend too hard that she had stars in her eyes.

They walked down the streets lined with strings of colored lights, hand in hand still. Her senses went on alert when he slowed.

"What is it?" She followed his gaze and saw the last row of houses that included their bed and breakfast. They were shrouded in darkness, some of them with dim, flickering lights coming from behind a window or two. At the bed and breakfast, two hurricane lamps flanked the steps.

"The power went out," the owner said as soon as they entered, handing them each a flashlight. "Probably too much ice on the wires."

"Thank you. We'll manage." Mike's voice was cordial, but she could see the tension in his body, in the way his large frame moved up the stairs ahead of her.

She hung back a few steps, giving him room to maneuver should he need to, guarding his back.

He listened at the door before opening it, swung the light in a wide arch as he entered. Empty. He lifted a hand when she would have followed, nodding toward the bathroom door. She nodded and waited.

He made quick work of his search. "It's okay."

She let the tension drain from her shoulders as she stepped forward, catching too late the movement behind her. The cold barrel of a gun pushed into the base of her skull and an iron fist closed around her arm as she was thrust forward.

Chapter Seven

Mike was blinded as the beam from Tessa's flashlight hit his face. He ducked at her call of warning, dropping his own light to grip his gun with both hands. He squinted, then froze the next second as he saw the outline of a man behind her and the gun at her head.

"Sit down," the man said, and Mike didn't need light to know who he was.

"Brady."

"Drop your gun and slide it toward me."

He did. He would have put it to his own head and pulled the trigger if Brady had asked. He would have done anything to keep the man from hurting Tessa.

Brady reached with his foot and kicked the gun well under the bed, out of sight. "Your knife."

"Let her go. She knows nothing," he said as he complied.

Brady made some sound through his nose. "Well, if she didn't before, she sure does now, doesn't she?" He looked at the fancy switchblade and pocketed it.

There were two chairs in the room, a lamp on the nightstand and a metal garbage can in the corner. Mike did the inventory without taking his eyes off the man, trying to think of anything he could use as a weapon, any trick he'd ever learned that would help him save Tessa.

"We'll do whatever you want us to do," he said, keeping his shoulders down, assuming the look of the beaten, the very picture of compliance.

"Very considerate of you. My wishes are very simple. Die fast. That about sums it up."

"You take your job too far. We weren't involved in anything. She was kidnapped by the smugglers, I came to get her because she means something to me. You know me. I'm too pigheaded to sit back and let someone else do a job I'm invested in. We butted heads over that before, re-member?"

"I remember all kinds of things about you, McNair."

"Look, we are the least of your worries on this. We're both military. She's army, I'm in a—" he paused a second "—I'm in a special unit. My security clearance is probably as high as yours. We're on the same team here."

"Not for this deal." His voice was as cold as the Arctic wind that tore down the street outside and rattled the windows. He'd made up his mind, that voice said, and he wasn't going to change it.

Mike's heart slammed against his chest. "If you shoot her, I'll reach you before you can squeeze off a second shot."

"There's that to consider." Brady didn't sound perturbed. He'd always been one cold son of a bitch. "I could, of course, always shoot you first and take my time with her."

Rage flooded Mike at the barely veiled threat. The lamp. The lamp on the night-stand was carved of some local stone. It would be heavy enough. Mike shifted his weight toward it.

"Do you really think it's a good idea to provoke me?"

"Do you think it's a good idea to shoot two innocent people just so you can look good at work and get your next promotion for cleaning up the Alaska mess?"

"Work." Brady snorted at the word. "It's not about the promotion. And as far as the authorities are concerned, you are hardly innocent. Your girlfriend here took off with the smugglers. The CIA took a nuclear warhead off your hands while you were shooting at their chopper."

"In self-defense."

Brady shrugged. "A point of view, isn't it?"

"If we're criminals, we should stand trial."

"Upholding the law is not one of my priorities just now."

What the hell was that supposed to mean?

"You were in on it." The words slipped from Mike's lips as the sudden realization hit him. "You're not covering for the government. You're covering your own ass."

Silence confirmed his words.

Fury filled him. "How could you? The other things, the money I could understand. But now this? Treason?"

"Shut the hell up! What do you know of treason?" Brady was losing his cool.

Good. Maybe he would make a mistake.

"I know selling nuclear weapons to another country qualifies."

The man shook his head. "One day you're fighting against an enemy, putting your life at risk, the next day the government tells you the people who'd tried their damnedest to slit your throat are now your friends and you have to make nice."

The Russians. That's what this was about. "Then why give the warheads to them?"

"Not to them," Brady snapped at him. "The Chechens."

And suddenly everything made horrifying sense.

"My enemy's enemy is my friend," Brady went on. "Remember Patrick?"

"Sure." Mike inched closer to the end table and the lamp. Patrick O'Donnell was the most decent person he had met during his short stint with the CIA.

"He got his shoulder busted. The bone is shot to slivers. The insurance company wouldn't pay for a replacement. They consider it cosmetic surgery. The man doesn't have a freaking shoulder." He shook his head. "You know how many times he'd risked his life for this country?"

"I'm sorry to hear about Patrick. I understand how you feel. You want to make sure whatever comes your way, you have enough money to handle it. Hell, I want the same. But do you really think this is the way to go about it?"

"Nobody gets hurt but our enemy."

Mike nodded, as if coming to understand the man's twisted logic. Trying to convince Brady that Russia was now an ally wouldn't get him anywhere. The warheads had been sold, Brady couldn't undo what he'd done. The only way out was to disarm him as fast as they could, then make sure they caught the boat to Uelen.

"Put these on." Brady tossed a pair of handcuffs onto the bed.

"Come on. It's not necessary. We were too late. We don't know scrap. Even for the things we think we know, we've got no proof."

He bristled against the idea of having his hands literally tied, the helplessness of it. No, he wouldn't be helpless, damn it. Thinking like that was the worst thing he could do. He would just be at a disadvantage. He could handle that. The more secure Brady felt, the more likely he was going to overlook something, make a mistake. Mike slipped on the cuffs and clicked them locked.

"Let's go." Brady pulled Tessa with him. "We are going out the back door. You first." He stepped aside.

Mike had no choice but to obey. As long as that gun was pressed against her head, nothing he could do would be as fast as Brady's finger on the trigger. But the man was taking them somewhere. That was good. Delay would hopefully bring an opportunity, and he only needed one chance. He would be ready for it.

He went down the stairs, careful not to

make too much noise, not wanting the owner or any of the boarders to be involved. Brady wouldn't hesitate to shoot if cornered. He'd gone too far to turn around now. Let him play out his plan, let him get comfortable, let him think everything was going just fine.

"There, sit in the very back." The man nodded toward a minivan that waited for them outside.

Mike did as he was told, squeezing into the third row, scanning it immediately. Nothing but a blanket. Hardly a formidable weapon. And the distance to the front was too great, a whole other row of seats between them. Brady kept Tessa next to him, on the passenger side, moving the gun from her head and pointing it at her chest.

"Let's not make this messy."

"Drop us off somewhere outside of town," Tessa said. "By the time we make it back, if we make it back, you'll be long gone. The authorities are looking for us. It'll be the word of two suspected criminals against a CIA agent."

"Shut up." Brady pulled out onto the road.

Patience. Mike sat back, resisting the urge to vault over the seats and rip the man's throat out. If he'd ever had need of a clear head, it was now. No room for his temper, no room for anything but a single attempt at saving their lives. He wouldn't get more than one chance, if that. He had to wait.

He watched the streets, relaxing a little when they passed the ones that turned down to the harbor. At least Brady's plans didn't involve the freezing water. Even a few minutes in the sea would be deadly this time of the year. But it looked like the man had another idea. He was driving out of town.

"Where are we going?" Mike asked when he felt he could do so without ticking him off.

"On the wilderness trail." Brady's voice was smug, with a smile in it. "They got three hundred miles of road just going off into nowhere for hunters and tourists and whoever else wants to see this godforsa- ken armpit of the world."

The wind whistled outside the car, the

darkness nearly complete once they were out of town, no streetlights here, no moon and stars, either. Snow clouds covered the sky. The van's headlights illuminated the road twenty or thirty feet in front of them, but beyond that there was nothing, as if they were driving into the end of the world, riding on the dark road to hell.

"I didn't plan on this. You got involved on your own. You could never leave well enough alone and mind your own business, McNair," Brady said, then turned on the radio, flipping through the channels before settling on an oldies station.

Was he having a last surge of conscience?

"It's not right. You know it isn't. A child is a child, whether American or Russian. Those warheads will be used to kill innocents."

"I have nothing to do with that. I'm not aiming any rockets."

"No. You're just tipping them with nuclear warheads. Is there a difference?"

"Damn right there is. I told you, it won't be our worry."

"Just drop us off." Mike tried again.

"We're far enough now. The weather will kill us, anyway. That way you won't have straight out murder on your hands."

"Out of all people—" Brady raised his voice over the soft music. "You should know, that I always cross my t's and dot my i's."

TESSA WRAPPED her arms around herself, shivering in the cold now that they had left the shelter of the car after a two-hour drive.

"Stop," Brady ordered, and she obeyed.

They were standing a good ten feet in front of the van, their bleak surroundings illuminated by the headlights. Brady wasn't hanging on to her anymore, probably figured she wouldn't be stupid enough to run. He was right. She wouldn't leave Mike behind. She pretended to stomp her feet for warmth and in the process moved a yard or so away.

"Get out," he directed Mike.

She watched Mike slide from the van and knew him well enough to know he would make his move as soon as he came close enough to Brady. She rolled her shoulders, prepared to lunge. If they jumped the man at the same time, he could shoot at only one of them before the other one reached him. Worst-case scenario: at least one of them would live. Best-case scenario: Brady would miss, or only wound with the shot.

Mike put his head down. He was ready. She lunged the same instant as he rushed forward.

Brady did get off a shot at Mike, apparently he'd judged him the bigger danger. But Tessa was on him, then Mike, too, the three of them rolling in the snow, trying to gain control of the weapon.

Pain shot up her arm as it got pinned under her, then the tangle of bodies rolled again and she was free.

The gun.

She got to it first, her hand on top of Brady's while Mike twisted the man's wrist to aim the weapon away from either of them. Her hood had come off, but she barely noticed the snow packing in the neck of her coat, stinging her cheeks. She fought with everything she had.

In the back of her mind she thought of Mike's knife in Brady's coat pocket. She couldn't afford to let go of the gun to reach for it. Not yet.

Brady had the weapon in a death grip. She moved her hand up a little, thinking to empty the magazine by squeezing the trigger and shooting off into the air until she rendered the weapon useless. She put her fingers over Brady's just as he and Mike heaved again, pulling against her. She'd had the trigger squeezed before she realized the whole mess of them were about to twist.

The gunshot echoed through the silence of the night, deafening in close proximity. For a moment she wasn't sure if the bullet had hit anyone and, if so, which one of them it was.

She felt no pain. Mike was moving. She rolled away and the weapon came with her, pulling from Brady's hand easily. His head flopped at the tug, and then she saw the hole in the side of his head and the blood spreading on the snow beneath it.

She looked away.

At one time she'd been trained for hand-to-hand combat, but it'd been a while since she'd had practice, two years since she'd fought anyone in earnest. Her legs were shaking when she got up.

Mike was already going through the man's clothes, pulling out Brady's cell phone and the switchblade. "Good work." He grinned at her. "Come on, we got a boat to catch." He tucked the gun away in his parka.

The boat. The warheads. Their mission was far from over.

Her mind zeroed in on the task ahead, and she ran to the van on Mike's heels without a glance at the body on the snow behind them.

"I drive, you call." He rattled off a number.

She dialed and listened to the automated voice that rendered the phone useless. "Password protected," she said.

"Keep it with you anyway." He shook his head as he stepped on the gas.

The terrain was flat, the road manage-able for now. Snow began to fall again, though, and it was coming down without mercy. The windshield wipers swished back and forth, the only sound as Mike concentrated on the road. He swore softly from time to time. She couldn't blame him. They still had a long way to go, and if the snow blocked the road, they were doomed. No snowplows would come this way until morning, if then. If the road was already considered closed for the year, no snowplows would come this way until spring.

Still, they might have been able to win against the snow. But they couldn't win against the caribou—not a whole herd of them.

With visibility being close to none, they didn't see the animals until it was too late. Mike swerved, but still hit at least one. Brakes screeched, finding no purchase on the icy road. The airbag smashed into her face, hot enough to burn. They came to a halt when the van crashed into a frozen snowbank.

"Couldn't life be easy just once?" she grumbled as she got out.

"If life was easy, this country wouldn't need people like us," he said.

It felt good to be counted in the same category with him.

"Are you okay?" he asked as he came after her.

"Fine. You're bleeding." She reached to the bloody spot on his cheekbone, but he shrugged, making light of it.

"Just a scratch."

They checked out the van together. The front end was smashed up badly.

"Damn."

"Let's give it a try." She walked back to the van, refusing to concede defeat, and turned the key in the ignition. Nothing. She let her head rest against the steering wheel for a moment before gathering herself and getting out. "How far are we from town?"

"Too far."

Which meant that, unless a good Samaritan drove by and offered them a lift within the next few minutes, there was no way they could make it to the harbor in time. And the chance of another vehicle on this remote road at this time was... There was no chance at all.

"Mike?"

He'd been staring at the crumpled hood, but his attention snapped to her.

"Where are the caribou? If we injured any, we should put them out of their pain."

He glanced around. "They're probably a ways down the road by now."

She peered through the darkness as far as she could see, but spotted no large shadows on the ground. She walked back to the road, found the spot where they'd had the accident and shook her head in wonder as she took in the jumble of hoof prints, not a drop of blood among them.

The reindeer had been lucky. She looked up as other animals came to mind.

"What?" Mike was watching her.

"You know how a few days ago you asked about polar bears and I said we weren't in their territory?"

He nodded cautiously.

"We are now," she said.

He took a few seconds to glance around before going back to the van and lifting the hood. He was clanging around for a while then gave up with a disgusted string of obscenities.

She walked back to him. "Let's get in the van while we figure something out." They had a long walk ahead of them. No sense in getting a head start on hypothermia.

He nodded and followed her.

"Let me see that phone," he said when they were both inside and the doors were closed behind them. He turned it on once she passed it over, played the buttons as if it were a video game.

"What are you doing?"

"Reprogramming it to get around the password."

"You can do that?"

He flashed her a smile that was close enough to his old cocky self to give her hope.

When he was done, he dialed, swore and flipped the phone closed then stuck it into his inside pocket.

"Didn't work?"

He turned to her with a raised eyebrow

as if slightly insulted. "No signal. Damn storm."

She turned on the dome light and squeezed into the back, looked around for anything that could be helpful. She picked up the blanket. They'd definitely take that. The tire iron, too, in case they came across any unfriendly wildlife. Mike had Brady's gun, but she wasn't sure what it had in the way of bullets.

She was crawling back to the front when the idea hit her. "Remember our first date?"

He looked at her with more than a little surprise. "What exactly here reminds you of Arizona?"

"This." She grinned and shoved the blanket at him. They'd gone windsurfing during their twenty-four-hour leave from desert training.

He caught on quick and his lips spread into a smile. "You're good."

"I try. What else do we need?"

"You get two tires off the van, I'll go find something for poles. Got anything useful on you?"

She shook her head. "Your emergency kit?"

"It's back at our room." He looked through the car, leaving no part of it unexplored. "If there were any trees out here, we'd be good," he said.

She struggled with the tires but was managing.

"I have another idea." He walked to the front of the car. "Forget the blanket. We'll have a solid sail."

He yanked on the hood. It gave, having been already damaged in the crash. When he was done, he pulled some tubing and wiring. Then they went to work on their contraption.

Mike placed the tire iron between the two tires to separate them and tied them on while she worked on securing their metal "sail." She glanced at her watch. It was eight thirty in the morning. They still had time. The boat was set to leave at first light, after ten.

They rigged the hood to the tires, then carried the whole thing over to the road. They each pushed a tire, running behind.

Mike pulled the "sail" standing, and with one hand, tied it off. The wind caught it just as they each jumped onto a tire. Then they were flying down the road, the smooth sides of rubber tires sliding easily on the frozen snow.

"Not too bad." She grinned from ear to ear.

"This baby knows speed." Mike grinned back at her.

They were making good progress, but getting colder and colder. The heat generated by their initial efforts wore off quickly, her good humor turning to thoughts of survival. They couldn't snuggle up now, or even wrap their arms around themselves. They each had to hold one side of the hood steady and into the wind, no matter how their arms ached, or how the wind whipped their backs.

They raced against time, the lives of thousands, perhaps tens of thousands in their hands.

She glanced over at Mike's hard-set face and felt a familiar tug on her heart. This was the Mike she had fallen for. He was the kind of man who would rush into danger if he thought he could help, without regard for race or nationality or religion. He would put <u>himself</u> on the line over and over, for people who needed to be saved.

He would go to Russia and try to get the warheads, even though if he got caught, he would be tried and imprisoned as a spy by the very people he was trying to save. But Mike wasn't the type of man to count personal risk when it came to a mission.

He had such a strength in him. It drew her and scared her at the same time, and how foolish was that, considering he had never once given her a reason to feel scared around him?

She had insisted on being treated as an equal, on making a team with him. But she hadn't wanted a true team. She'd wanted two separate independent entities who happened to work and live together.

A real team meant more. The last couple of days they'd spent fighting for survival taught her that. A real partnership meant interdependence instead of independence.

And for the first time, she started to consider that maybe it wasn't a weakness.

If they got out of this mess alive— She had a hard time finishing the thought. She wasn't sure if she could walk away from Mike again, wasn't sure if she wanted to. But the only alternative was putting her heart on the line again. Could she do that? Or was it already too late? Was she just pretending to still have power over that decision?

NOT A MOMENT TO LOSE. Mike caught sight of one of the Russian fishermen pulling in the last rope, their boat slipping away from the dock. They were almost there. Just a little more. He walked as fast as he could without drawing attention. They lucked out in that department. The Nome harbor was nearly deserted. Two men stood talking at the far end, paying attention to little else other than the argument between them.

He watched the sailor wind up the rope.

"Come on, get inside," he murmured to the sole man on deck, as if he could some-how send him a mental message.

They moved out of the shelter of the crates that lined the street. The wind had died down, but it was still snowing a little, and the cold was biting with full force.

There was a four-foot gap now between the boat and the dock, five feet, six feet and growing.

The man finally slipped inside the pilot's house. Mike ran and jumped without hesitation, the boat big enough that he didn't rock it. Tessa was making a run for it, following him.

No. Too late. The dock was too far now.

Relief filled him for a second. She would have to stay behind, stay safe.

But instead of slowing down, she picked up speed and flew off the end of the dock, her arms flailing as she swooshed through the air.

His heart stopped. Blood rushed loudly in his ears. The water. She was going to hit the water.

The next second he was lurching over the edge, reaching for her, prepared to go in if he had to. He didn't. He managed to catch her by the top of her fingers. He grabbed for her wrist, needing a better grip, then pulled her up, and for a second crushed her to his chest, and just held her there, unable to talk or do anything more.

If either of them had had their gloves on, he would have lost her to the icy, churning water. The thought tore through his brain and he hugged her tighter still. "Don't you ever—" He started to say, but then just shook his head and let her go.

There was no time to be mad at her for taking such a risk. They had to get out of sight before the man in the pilot house looked back. He opened the lid of the cargo hold and slid down first to make sure it was safe before signaling Tessa to follow him.

A fair-size space waited for them below. He made a more thorough inspection once his eyes got used to the dark and he could see farther. Crates and packages were piled high everywhere. Tessa moved first, and he followed her all the way to the back where they were least likely to be discovered if any of the crew came down.

They could hear men talking on the other

side of a thin wooden wall where the cargo hold joined the crew's cabin. He figured four or five of them, judging by the voices. It confirmed what he'd determined the day before, watching them coming and going from the boat.

He looked at Tessa, making a signal, and she nodded as she sat on a large crate, understanding his unspoken message. If they could hear the men, that meant the men would hear them. They would have to make the trip in silence. They couldn't risk being discovered. The weapons smugglers were a day ahead of them, in Uelen already, prepared to move deeper into Siberia.

Chapter Eight

She was dying.

She didn't hate the general feeling of misery as much as she hated her helplessness. That really ticked her off.

The boat rocked violently from side to side, the waves crashing above them as they washed over the deck. Tessa heaved, but nothing came up. Her stomach had been emptied hours ago.

Mike had cleaned up her mess and found some water for her to rinse her mouth.

He sat next to her on top of the large crate where she was sprawled out on her back, and held her head on his lap. He smoothed her hair out of her face with long, gentle fingers.

"Feeling any better?"

She didn't have the strength to answer.

Her first time on a boat. She hoped it would be the last. If she'd had the strength for it, she would have felt embarrassed. Here she'd been trying to prove how tough and strong she was, how no obstacle could get in her way when she was on a mission, and she'd been undone, undone to the point of defenselessness, by some choppy water. All she could do was moan when the boat pitched again and her stomach flipped over.

The place smelled musky, a mixture of seawater and old wood, and other smells left behind by various cargoes of the past. She turned her head and pressed her face to Mike's leg, inhaled his familiar scent of sweat and maleness that was neither sharp nor unpleasant, reminding her of cedar wood. She closed her eyes to pretend they were on solid ground.

The small pup tent her imagination brought forth wasn't a huge stretch from the dark belly of the ship. Mike and she had been a team, each carrying half of the tent during the endless exercises, sharing it, huddled in their separate sleeping bags at night.

He'd been trying to get into her pants for months by then, so had half of the platoon. Except that, unlike with the rest of the men, she *was* attracted to Mike, and to more than his quick, lethal smile and combat-honed body.

They were all tough and brave, but Mike was more. You got to know a man when you fought side by side with him. He had honor and a surprising side of gentleness that came out at the oddest moments and took her breath away.

And yet she'd ignored whatever it was that drew her to him. She hadn't wanted to be wanted because she was the only woman in sight.

She remembered the night when that had changed, when she'd finally come to him. They had done really well that day, and they talked about strategy, making plans for the morning. She'd been so optimistic and grateful for getting a partner who didn't resent her presence there, who was open-minded enough to give her a chance. Not all of the five provisional female recruits had been that lucky.

She had thrown her arms around his neck and brushed her lips over his, just about jumping with excitement, meaning it a gesture of… Well, however she had meant it wasn't the way he had taken it. His arms locked around her like a steel cage, his lips crushing down on hers so suddenly that she had panicked, pulled back and butted her head with full force against his mouth to make him release her.

He had, swearing as he stepped away.

She had drawn her arm back, ready to follow up with her best hook to the soft of his stomach, but the look in his eyes had stopped her, as had the drop of blood that rolled off his split lip.

Her own lips had still burned from his kiss.

"I'm sorry," he had said. "I didn't mean to scare you."

"You didn't." She'd drawn herself up. Admitting to being scared went against her grain.

"I thought you wanted to."

"I didn't."

He'd nodded, then looked at her warily when she stepped closer, but all she'd done was wipe off the drop of blood. Her fingertips had tingled where she'd touched his lips, the strange sensation running up her arms and tightening her nipples.

She *had* been scared, and it had infuriated her. She'd hated the weakness of it. But beyond the panicky urge to flee, another sensation blossomed in her body and it proved hard to ignore.

"I want to now," she had said to prove she wasn't afraid of anything, and brushed her lips gently over his swollen one. She'd kissed him and he'd let her, allowing her to take as much or as little as she had wanted. He had kept his hands by his sides.

Her body had been humming with need by the time she was done. "I want more," she had said, and he had given a strangled laugh.

"If I touch you, are you going to try to maim me?"

"Scared?" She had turned the tables on him.

"Nah. I'm thinking it's worth the risk."

He had kissed her then, softly, but making it clear he meant it.

When his hands had stolen up her arms, she hadn't pulled away, not even when his palms cupped her aching breasts.

"I've never done this before," she'd murmured against his lips.

He had drawn away. "Are you sure you want to? With me?"

She had nodded, unable to say the words.

He'd nodded back solemnly and kissed her again.

He hadn't taken her—they had taken each other. It had been petrifying and glorious at the same time, small drops of pain mixed in with an ocean of pleasure.

God, it seemed like a million years ago.

The boat rolled again, and Tessa's fingers curled into Mike's thigh, the contact bringing her back from the past. Her stomach seemed a little more settled, probably because she had managed to keep her mind off her wretched state for a while.

He bent to her ear, his warm breath

tickling her earlobe when he spoke. "Feeling any better?"

The clamor of the storm was loud enough to drown out any other noise, so they no longer had to worry about detection, but still they kept to whispering.

She nodded hesitantly.

"I didn't realize this would be your first time on a ship."

"If you say one more time how you wish you'd left me behind in Nome, I'm going to gather up enough strength to hit you if it kills me."

He lifted her left hand and massaged the area between her wrist bones. "It's supposed to help with nausea," he said.

She let him, not because she believed anything on this earth could help her, but because she didn't want to waste energy by protesting.

When he was done with the left hand, he moved on to the right, the gentle pressure of his fingertips warming her skin. His rhythmic caresses felt nice, distracting her from her misery if nothing else.

"Better?"

"Maybe." She made some noncommittal sounds.

"Let me try the feet." He pulled off her mukluks and put them next to her parka that he had helped her out of earlier to keep it out of harm's way.

He tried massaging through her socks for a few seconds before he pulled them off, frustrated. She didn't need them; she wasn't cold. The crew's cabin next to them had some kind of a stove, and heat radiated through the wall.

"I'm not sure what the right spot is here, so I'm just going to go over everything. Let me know if something works."

He started with her toes and massaged them until they were tingling. He moved on to the ball of her foot, then to the arch. He caressed the hollow below her ankle, alternating pressure with lighter strokes.

The storm was quieting outside, but inside her, sensations swirled that made her forget everything but his touch.

"Better now?"

"Yes."

"Want me to stop?"

"No."

She had forgotten her seasickness a while back. Pleasure radiated up her body now from every spot he touched. He had noticed the change in her, too, his caresses growing suggestive and sensuous.

She bit back a sigh. She was only letting him do this because she was going to die, anyway, no sense of dying miserable instead of happy if she had the choice.

A few minutes passed before she realized she might not have a choice after all. Her body was making its intentions crystal clear, her blood humming with need.

"I don't remember you being this solic- itous before," she said. "One of the scores of women you've had since I last saw you taught you good." Some of the pain returned at the thought.

"Scores?" He crooked an eyebrow.

True. What had she been thinking. It had been three full years. "More?"

He shook his head.

It was a stupid game. She didn't want to know. "Ten?" She pulled her feet from his grasp.

He shook his head again.

"Four?" She'd had four lovers since him, although she had trouble believing he would restrict himself to that few. Her first had been to prove that she was over Mike. The second to erase the memory of the disastrous first. The third to prove that she could have another relationship and not still yearn after the man who'd broken her heart. She gave up after that third one. George had been unplanned and unexpected, friendship trying to stretch into more between two lonely people who got along well in every other regard.

"There hasn't been anyone," he said so quietly she barely caught it above the noises of the sea.

She couldn't have been more surprised if he'd confessed that he was an alien. Or more disbelieving.

It had to be a line. An angle he was working. "Right, tell me another one."

He stayed quiet, but she could see his shoulders stiffen.

"I'm sorry," she whispered, truly stunned now. "It's just that—"

"Never mind," he said, and pulled away.

Mike McNair had lived three years of celibacy because of her. It boggled the mind. She wouldn't have thought it possible, unless there'd been a disabling accident.

A funny feeling spread through her chest cavity.

"I'm sorry," she said again. "For everything."

"Me, too, Tessa." He reached out a hand, but dropped it before he reached her.

"Touch me."

He stepped up to her head and drew a finger down her cheek, then stopped.

"Like before."

He picked up her hand and started to massage it again.

"No, like before before." She pulled her hand away. And from the slow smile that spread across his face, she knew he finally understood what she was talking about.

A look passed between them, crackling with tension, passions awakening.

"It's been too long, you might have to show me." His voice was thick.

He was teasing her now. She'd be damned if she would let him have the upper hand this once. She sat up to face him, let her fingers learn his face all over again. He watched her with an intensity that took her breath away but did not reach for her. She grew uncertain for a moment and buried her face in the warm nook of his neck.

Her lips touched muscles that were taut with tension. He was holding his body in iron control. She smiled against his skin, her will rising to the challenge, her body forgetting about the rolling waves beneath them.

Her hands slid up his chest, over the planes of muscles, then dipped down to get under the clothes that separated his burning skin from her fingertips. His flat nipples hardened into rock, and he bit back a groan when she skimmed over them.

She let her hands roam where they might, let her fingers slide through the silky hairs that covered him, while she tasted the salty skin of his neck.

The past three years disappeared. Old

passions slammed into her hard, crumbling her defenses, bringing back feelings she'd long buried if not forgotten.

"Tessa?" He whispered against her hair, his hot breath fanning the patch of exposed skin behind her ears, sending a delicious shiver across her skin.

Her response was to move closer, until her breasts pressed against his chest, her body seeking as much contact as their position allowed.

"Tessa," he said again as his arms finally came around her.

She kissed the strong line of his jaw, the corner of his mouth, his cheeks, his closed eyelids, and in turn he did the same, responding in equal, but never pushing for more.

His control infuriated her now.

Damn him that he could still hold back, because she couldn't. She was past the point of reason.

She bit his earlobe, waiting for his arms to lift her up and lay her down, wanting him to take her the way she had remembered, hard and fast, taking no prisoners.

He had always been gentle when needed, when they'd both been in the mood for it. But at other times… He'd been fireworks, dynamite, searing flashes of heat that drove her over the edge. She had missed their fiery joinings that used to leave her body aching.

That was what she wanted now. She wanted to be possessed and possess in return. She wanted oblivion. She wasn't a delicate flower, damn it.

But instead of the mad rush she was craving, he took her earlobe into his mouth, scraped it with his teeth before settling in to suckle it slowly. He was driving her mad.

She reached for the hem of her pullover and yanked it over her head together with the long-sleeved shirt beneath, separating herself from Mike but a moment before her lips were plastered against his.

The air in the cabin that was comfortable enough when she'd been fully dressed now nipped at her naked skin, the heat of his palms when they found her rib cage, a shock.

She had to tug at his clothes more than once before he pulled them off and she was finally settled against his warmth, skin to skin. She took a slow breath, let it out little by little.

"I missed this." The admission slipped out before she could bite her lips.

"Me, too." He dipped his head and buried his face between her breasts.

She arched her back as she reached for the clasp of her bra, pushing her tender skin into his rough beginnings of a beard, a sensation that sent her nerve endings singing and her skin tingling with pleasure.

He rubbed his face all over her, making small noises in the back of his throat. Her knees were trembling. She hugged his waist with her thighs and locked her legs together behind his back, bringing them into full contact, his unmistakable hardness pressed against her.

She squeezed her eyes together and let her head fall back, and the next moment his hot mouth found her puckered nipple. His wet heat drew her in until she thought she would melt onto his lap.

Her fingers slipped through his short hair, down to his wide shoulders, gliding over corded muscles that rose and disappeared like waves as he moved. He let go of the nipple, blew on it gently, then after a moment, when it was aching with the pain of needing to be touched, he claimed it again, tugging on it, suckling with force, scraping it with his teeth until she thought she would go mad.

And then he moved over to the other one.

Blood was rushing to the vee of her thighs where she felt swollen, wet and ready to burst.

Not yet, not yet. If he could control his body, then she could control hers. She would not be the first to capitulate.

She leaned back until she was lying down, needing to put a moment of distance between them so she could regroup. Not to happen. His burning gaze caressed her skin as effectively as the most skilled seducer's touch.

"You could kill a man," he said.

She watched his chest rise and fall.

"That's what we've been trained for." She didn't want to talk about the army now.

"I meant with wanting."

He moved his body until he was above her, suspended on his arms, lying between her legs.

He dipped his head and placed a row of kisses along her crooked collarbone first, then the straight one. The gesture brought to mind the incident that had broken the bone, her wrestling match with the alligator the day her Special Forces career had ended before it began.

"Let it go," he whispered into her neck, reading her mind.

She had to, because the next moment he was dragging his whiskers across her skin, enveloping her in a haze of lust. He'd just been pretending that she was dominating this encounter. He'd been fighting all along. And he wasn't fighting fair.

She lifted her hips and slid against his hardness, gratified at the sound of his breath catching in his throat. Not enough. She slipped her hands under his waistband and cupped his bare buttocks.

He answered by grinding himself into her, making it her turn to gasp for air.

When his lips returned to her breasts, she squirmed with need and squeezed a hand between her pelvis and his, and once he figured out what she was about, he allowed her more room, enough for the second hand.

She tried to make quick work of her pants, but her fingers kept fumbling. She undid the snaps and the zipper and tugged the edges open, but could not pull the things down. Mike's hands were lost in her hair and rather than wait for him to mirror her actions, she went to work on his clothes next.

When she loosened his pants, she pushed her hands under the fabric and shoved it off together with the boxer briefs, twisting, trying to align their bodies. Then the core of his heat sprang against her naked skin, rigid and swollen, and for a moment she froze as her body soaked in the sensation.

His head moved up until he could look into her eyes. She wasn't sure what he found there, but he moved away.

"No," she reached for him weakly, as he came to stand at the end of the crate that was now covered with their clothing.

Her mouth went dry at the sight of his nakedness. She had forgotten how big he was, or rather, she had thought the memory was an exaggeration. He had a warrior's body, and hers had no trouble recalling the things it used to do to her. She felt a gush of wetness that came to prepare his entry, an entry he might yet very well refuse.

But he grabbed on to her ankles and pulled her down until her knees bent and her feet dangled over the side of the crate. Then his fingers crept up her inner thigh and tightened on her flesh as he took hold of her once again and pulled her further down, leaving her with her buttocks resting on the edge, her knees pushed up now, one warm large hand of his behind each of her trembling thighs, his fingers splayed wide.

His gaze held her spellbound then it slid down over her body, and he pushed her legs apart, opening her to him. The muscles in his face and shoulders shifted, but she could no longer feel embarrassed, nor could she summon her old will to fight.

What would she fight against?

He had mastered her body and she had mastered his. The proof was as stiff as carved granite between them, if she needed any proof of his wanting.

He came closer, until he was pushing against her sensitized bottom, but he did not angle himself to enter her, content instead with leaving their bodies pressed against each other. He moved his arms and supported her legs with his body, seeking for his fingers a new occupation.

He parted her flesh with his thumb, finding the core of her pleasure unerringly and resting his fingertip against it lightly. When she squirmed, he increased the pressure, then let up, then increased it again. She felt her juices seep from her body and arched her back, shameless as she sought her release.

He responded by changing the rhythm and switching from pressure to circling. That nearly did her in. She was trembling on the edge when he pulled back. She bit her lip. She had given herself to him fully. He would not make her beg. She would not, if it killed her.

He eased back and she missed the heat and hardness of his body. Then she raised her heavy-lidded gaze to his face and realized he was no longer watching her, but was looking intently at the wall. And then she heard it, men talking on the other side. The storm had died down.

How long ago? Had she made any loud noises? Had the crew heard?

She let her feet slide down the side of the crate, her body pulsating with need and disappointment, grieving the absence of Mike's. She had to get ahold of herself and get dressed. He caught her knees and stepped between them, slowly shaking his head. He didn't have to tell her to be quiet.

This time he parted her with two fingers and allowed them to slide down after a brief tease. He stroked her lobes, outlining her opening, circling over and over again as a second finger joined the first and the two glided around her sensitized entrance that was wet with her welcome.

She could think of little else but his entering.

Soon. He had to. He was only human. He couldn't torture her endlessly. At one point his own body would need release more than he could hold back.

He brought her to the edge several times just to stop, one time going as far as opening her folds fully and bending to blow cold air on her innermost parts to cool them. She wondered if the last three years she had spent by trying to replace him with other men, he had spent by planning his revenge.

Then he finally shifted again and pressed his hard tip against her wet core. She squirmed to hurry him, but he wouldn't have it, holding her hips in place, his fingers biting into her flesh. Slowly he pushed forward, opening her to him as he inserted the very tip, but only until the ridge was in, then stopped. The walls of her body closed around him, trying to pull him deeper, but he resisted. He wiggled, just a little, and she opened her mouth to gasp at the bone-melting pleasure of it, but he leaned forward swiftly and sealed her lips before she could make a sound.

She couldn't make any noise. She could not cry out, no matter what he did to her, or she would risk discovery by the men on the other side of the thin plank wall. She had to remember that.

He held her bottom lip between his teeth and rubbed his chest over her breasts, his silky hair teasing her nipples into hard points of need. He obliged them by rounding his back and closing a warm lip over one, reaching up with one hand to roll the other between his thumb and forefinger.

He pulled the part of him that she wanted the most at the moment, until the ridge cleared her opening, then eased it back again, sucking hard on her nipple at the same time. And just as she felt her muscles quiver, getting ready to contract, he pulled up to standing, leaving her wet nipples hard in the cold air.

The Russians had some music on and were singing in their cabin. The blood was rushing in her ears so loudly, she could barely hear them. When had they started that party?

Mike's hands were on her hips. He was poised at her opening, waiting. Damn it, would he make her beg?

She was beyond pride. "Please." She mouthed the word.

And still he didn't move. "Why?" He mouthed back, then bent to her ear. "To take your mind off being seasick?"

"Because I need you," she whispered, stunned just how much of that raw need reflected in her voice.

"And?" He drew out the moment, bringing them face-to-face, his dark gaze looking to her soul.

"What more do you want from me?" She could not give more, didn't he understand? She could not give her heart.

He took a deep breath and the next moment he sank into her to the hilt.

He filled her to bursting, stretching her. Heat radiated from her core; waves of pleasure rippled through her body. Her fingers sought purchase on the crate as he took her like a man who meant the taking.

He mastered her with long slow strokes, grinding himself into her with each.

They were afloat on a rising wave, higher and higher, coming in with the tide. Then the wave crested, leaving her dizzy and spent, lying with her bones gone soft as pleasure licked at her shores.

He pulled her up and gathered her to him, his arms closing tight around her, his face buried in her hair. She could feel his heartbeat against her cheek, beating as madly as her own.

She felt spent, depleted, too much so to analyze what had happened between them, her brain still steeped in too much pleasure to consider regret or implications. She tightened her arms around him and let go any nudging worry, taking a few selfish moments to enjoy the way her body was still tingling from his.

His muscles went taut, and she almost laughed. No way. Not again. He couldn't possibly mean— Then she heard the noise, too, and stiffened in alarm. Footsteps vibrated the wood planks above them.

Mike swept her to the floor, pulling their

clothes from the crate with his free hand just as the cargo hold hatch opened. She held her breath, grappling for clothes silently, then abandoning the effort. If it came to a fight, her nakedness might distract her opponent. It might give her a moment of advantage.

Mike handed her their only gun, crouching next to her as bare-skinned as she was. Lord, they made a pair. A smile stretched her lips. He looked at her and grinned back, gave a what-can-you-do shrug.

She couldn't see the stairs from where they were, way in the back, but she could hear boots stomp on wood as someone came down.

WHERE THE HELL was Brady? He was supposed to check in by now. His cell phone was set on voice mail. It didn't look like he'd been checking it. The Boss slammed the receiver down. He had already left three messages.

The last time he had talked to Brady, the man was going to take care of their little problem. Didn't look like that worked out. At this point the odds were that Brady had failed.

Damn Mike McNair. Why couldn't he pick up his girlfriend, take her back to the nearest hotel room and screw her brains out? Where the hell did they get off, deciding they were on a mission to save the world?

Somebody had to teach those two to mind their own business. He was just the man to do it.

All he had to do was find them.

It was too much to hope that Brady took them out on the ice fields and the reason he hadn't reported back was because polar bears ate all three of them. Brady's loss would be a bonus, if indeed that was how things had gone down. He would have had to take care of the man, anyway. He'd been a decent enough partner, but leaving loose ends was never a smart thing to do. If Mike, or a disgruntled polar bear, took care of Brady, so much the better.

The warheads were out of the U.S. He was as good as in Belize. He would see to the safe delivery of the goods then go to the sunshine that awaited him a couple of thousand miles to the south.

Finding Mike and Tessa shouldn't be too hard. If they were alive they would be following the transport. Which meant, all he had to do was wait. Sooner or later they would come to him.

Chapter Nine

Tessa held her breath as the man came down the steps and stopped. One person only, judging by the sound.

She stayed absolutely still, gripping the gun, hidden behind rows and rows of crates. They should be okay. He might go the other way, in any case.

He didn't.

Her muscles stiffened in alarm as his boots scraped the wood nearer and nearer. It wasn't that they couldn't handle the man between the two of them, but if they took out this one, complications would quickly follow.

She relaxed her shoulders then her entire body, keeping her muscles ready to move if she had to lunge at him and take him down. Mike had his knife. She gripped Brady's gun, although shooting the man would be their last resort.

If they shot him, the others would hear, then Mike and she wouldn't have any other choice but to take over the whole boat. Without the original crew, they would have to bring the boat to port themselves. And then how would they explain that to the port authorities when they docked?

They had to remain hidden.

The man came closer, no more than a row or two of crates between them now, close enough that the light of his lamp reached them. He stopped. Maybe he was looking for something. She hoped he would find it and wouldn't need to come any farther.

If he did, if he saw them, their best bet was the knife. They would have to take him quietly and hope his buddies didn't notice he was missing until after they reached port. Not much chance of that on a boat this size.

Why the hell did he have to come now?

The man was moving around, setting her nerves on edge with anticipation. She stared at the gap between the crates where he would be coming through if he decided to head this way.

Mike shifted silently next to her and put a hand on her knee. He could probably feel her body vibrate. She took a slow breath as he squeezed gently, allowing the warmth and strength of his fingers to relax her. He was trying to tell her that she wasn't alone in this mess, that they would be all right.

She nodded without looking at him, not daring to take her eyes off the gap between the rows.

He was coming.

Mike and she pulled back simultaneously into the narrow spot between their crate and the wall. Their bunched-up clothes lay at their feet. She glanced around. Nothing hung out. They were still okay, as long as the man didn't decide to look behind their crate.

The air still carried the scent of their lovemaking she realized and felt a moment of panic. Could he smell them?

His feet sounded heavier on the wood, as if he were carrying something. He was, the loud thump of some kind of box being dropped onto their crate confirmed it. He walked back, brought over the lamp.

For sure he would see them now. Tessa crouched as low to the ground as she could, trying to melt into the floor and, at the same time, maintain a position from which she could come up swiftly, take the man before he could get out a warning shout to his friends.

He grunted instead, and wood creaked. He was working on opening the box.

Seconds flew by, then minutes. Dust floated through the air, but she didn't dare sneeze. She didn't dare reach up to pinch the bridge of her nose, either, a trick to make the urge pass. The slightest movement might give them away.

They waited, frozen as motionless as two ice carvings until the man finally picked up his lamp and walked away. They didn't get up until the hatch door rattled closed behind him.

"What is it?" she whispered, feeling

around in the box the man had left open. Her fingers closed around a small can.

Some time passed before their eyes got used to the darkness again and they could make out the label.

"Ravioli," Mike said, and set a can on the crate to jab his knife into it.

The wind and waves picked up again outside, enough to mask the sound as he opened the can. She dressed, then took the food when he offered it, but she couldn't eat. The smell of tomato sauce mixing with the musky smells of the cargo hold was too much for her already-unhappy stomach. It roiled again, and she handed back the can.

"No, thanks."

He nodded and made quick work of the rest of the ravioli once he was done putting on his clothes. She looked away. Even the sound of his swallowing bothered her.

She'd been fine while they'd been making love, her attention thoroughly diverted, and again as they'd crouched behind the crate ready to attack, with her mind focused on the danger and forgetting her body. Now she noticed the sway of the ship again, and the sensation weakened her knees.

"How much longer?"

He shook his head. "Can't be long now," he said, and put down the can to fold his arms around her.

They stayed that way for what seemed years before a rush of activity above deck told them they were finally coming to port.

THEY WERE IN UELEN.

Mike waited in a crouch behind a pile of smaller crates beneath the stairs, Tessa to his right. He focused on the sounds above: men moving around and talking, feet shuffling on wood. But while his brain was tuned to their mission, his body was tuned to Tessa, aware of her nearness, still buzzing with the amazing lovemaking they had shared.

She'd been worth the wait, not that he was foolish enough to believe that she would come around now to accept that there was no man for her but him, just as for him there could be no other woman. She had given her body, but she wasn't ready yet to give her heart. That he had to win back still or spend his life trying.

The boat rocked slightly as the men tied it to the wharf. Footsteps scraped the deck, coming toward the hatch door above them. One man only. With luck, he would go to the back, and they would be out of here and off the ship before anyone noticed. In case the man came snooping in their direction, Mike had the gun ready. A well delivered blow to the head should give them enough time to get away.

The door rattled, and he readied himself, but instead of the hatch opening and feet appearing on the stairs, he heard the distinct click of metal above. The footsteps faded away.

They waited and listened. The only sounds now were the waves gently lapping against the hull and the occasional bump of the boat against the dock.

"What happened?" Tessa whispered after a few minutes.

"I think they left the unloading to the morning." He stood and walked over to the stairs, stepped up enough so that he could reach the door above him, pushed against it carefully at first, then with more force. It didn't budge more than an inch.

"Padlocked," he said. "They must have locked up the ship against thieves."

"Can you shoot off the lock?" She had come up behind him.

"I could, but there must be some port authority around. It's one of the nearest Russian ports to the U.S. I'm guessing it's guarded, especially at night. We shouldn't make any more noise than we have to."

"We can't wait. Can we break over to the crew's cabin?"

"If they locked this door, they would have locked that one, too."

She stepped away from him toward the wall. It was too dark to see her once she moved a couple of feet away, but he could hear her moving around.

"What are you doing?"

"Looking for a window."

Of course. He went to do the same, scanning the wall, feeling for any opening. And then he found it. "Here."

The porthole was on the starboard side,

disappointing in both its location and size. No way his shoulders could squeeze through that. "Anything over there?"

"Nothing." Tessa was coming to his side. "This is it."

"Too small," he said.

She fiddled with the latch and opened it. The cold sea air rushed in to hit them in the face. "Not for me."

"I'm not letting you go alone." Over his dead body.

"I can climb up to the deck and open the hatch for you."

"Do you know how cold this water is?"

"I don't need to know. I don't plan on falling."

"Mmph."

"You have to trust me."

"I do."

"Then give me a hand up." She stripped off her parka.

And in a moment of insanity he helped her out, regretting it as soon as she caught on to the railing and he saw her feet dangle outside the window for a long soul-freezing moment before she swung up to relative safety. He followed her movements by the sound of her boots on the deck, picturing where she was, what she was doing. He stood under the hatch door when she got over there, waited patiently while she fiddled with the lock.

"It's not going to work," she whispered down the crack. "I'm going to see if I can find a crowbar."

"Good idea," he said, and felt the boat sway slightly as she pushed away to jump to the dock.

No! Damn it. She was *not* supposed to leave the boat. What was wrong with looking for a crowbar right here? He went up the steps and heaved against the door with newfound strength. What on earth was she thinking?

You have to trust me, she had said. He was pretty sure the white-knuckled terror he was experiencing at the moment didn't qualify as trust, exactly. He took a deep breath, then another. She'd had some of the same training as he had. Nobody in their right mind would call Tessa Nielsen a defenseless woman.

Still, he couldn't sit still doing nothing. He went back and found the empty ravioli can, emptied his bursting bladder into it then stashed the can in a corner. Much relieved after that, he walked from crate to crate, prying the tops open, looking for any tool that would aid his escape. The first crate he tried contained more canned food; the second, boxes of laundry detergent. Looked like the fishermen didn't waste their involuntary visit to Nome and packed up whatever they could trade well back home.

Except, port authority and customs would never let them bring in this quantity of goods. The thought stilled his hands. The men must have planned on getting their loot off the boat before morning inspection. Which meant they'd probably gone off to get a truck or some other form of transportation. And they could be back any minute.

As if to confirm his worst fears, boots thumped onto the deck, footsteps coming straight for the hatch. He moved as close as he could while still staying in cover.

Metal clinked on metal, wood creaked

above, followed by a loud pop, then the next second the door flipped open. He sat on his haunches, ready to pounce on whoever came down those stairs. Mukluks came first, hardly distinguishable.

"Mike," the intruder whispered into the darkness.

He relaxed. "I'm here." He stepped from behind the crates and locked her in a bear hug.

"All right, now. Don't get all mushy on me." She punched him in the shoulder when he let her go. She shrugged into her parka. "We better haul ass."

Apparently, they hadn't been fast enough.

They met the returning crew as soon as they came up from the cargo hold. The men were in the process of boarding the boat, the surprise about equal on each side.

He stepped back immediately and Tessa followed, backing down the stairs. He made a motion with his hand in front of his mouth, signaling her to be quiet. Under no circumstances could they let on that they were American.

It would make a world of a difference afterward what the crew reported to the authorities—two thieves from the village, or two stowaway American spies. They might not even bother to report thieves, especially if they realized nothing was missing, that they had been in time to prevent being robbed.

They came down, four big men, swearing in Russian, their voices menacing but kept low. They didn't seem to want the attention of the port authority, either. They probably thought the four of them were more than enough to fend off a pair of starved thieves from the village.

Mike had the first one knocked out and on the ground the second he'd cleared the stairs. That made the rest more wary. They kept shoulder to shoulder as they backed away to give themselves enough room to maneuver.

THEY WERE TALKING in Russian, scolding, Tessa thought, not understanding the words. Their gestures looked threatening, as if they were trying to shoo the thieves up the stairs and off the ship. Apparently, their confidence in whupping the opposition had fallen with their unfortunate comrade.

She glanced at Mike, and he shook his head.

He was right. They couldn't go. They had to make sure the men wouldn't sound the alarm. Things were bad enough already, they couldn't risk further delay.

She squared her shoulders and caught the gun Mike tossed her. He opened the switchblade and set his feet apart, bent at the knees.

The men backed off farther, quiet now. They were unarmed.

And unwilling to give up their loot.

The largest of them rushed Mike, knocking him into the wall.

The other two, realizing she was reluctant to use her gun, came after her.

Man, oh, man. She really didn't want to have to hurt them. They weren't what she'd been trained to fight, terrorists or enemy combatants. They were just fishermen, their families waiting for them at home. Even if she could have used her weapon without attracting the attention of the port guards, she would have had a hell of a time justifying killing these men. They'd done nothing to deserve being shot, their only misfortune being that their boat had been in the wrong place at the wrong time.

She fought back with all she had.

Wearing a fur parka was no advantage in hand-to-hand combat, limiting her range of motion. On the other hand, it did soften the blows that came at her with disconcerting regularity from two sides. Unfortunately, it softened her impact as well. Elbowing one of the men in the stomach didn't even faze him. With all the padding on her, it probably felt as if she'd hit him with a pillow.

She tucked her gun away and put all her focus into pushing her attackers into retreat. As long as she was merely defending herself, they had the upper hand. She had to turn that around, to take out one then the other. From the corner of her eye she could see Mike rolling on the floor with the third man.

She struck out over and over again, but

the men attacking her were no slouches. Apparently, hauling in nets that weighed a ton had a way of putting muscle on a person.

She neutralized one with a powerful chop to the side of the head. Rather than taking heed, the other guy came at her with even more conviction.

Damn, she was tired. All that seasickness had worn her out. She could no longer see Mike. He and the other man had moved out of her range of vision, the only reminder of their presence an occasional grunt. She gathered her breath and charged forward with full steam, catching her opponent off guard.

They tangled and fell to the floor with a painful thud, she on the bottom. Luck wasn't with her on this trip so far. She hoped that would change quickly.

She saw movement from the corner of her eye as she struggled to get the man under her, spotted Mike at last, standing alone, breathing hard. He made no move to help her.

Oh, hell. The extra splash of fury was

just enough to push her over the edge. She brought her fist up and hooked the guy with full force, sending him sprawling next to her. He didn't get up.

She lay there, gasping for air for a minute.

Mike came over and offered his hand. *Now,* he was all Mr. Let-Me-Help? She flashed him her best "evil" look.

"I could have used that hand a few minutes ago," she snapped at him as she got up on her own.

"Who are you kidding?" He drew up his eyebrows. "If I took over, you would have wanted to kick my ass."

He bent to take the belt off the man at his feet, and tied the guy's hands with it.

She shrugged, then went to help him with the next fisherman. "It's harder to beat four Russians unconscious than I thought."

"You don't know the half of it. When I was in Siberia before, there was this one guy—" He fell silent. "I think they grow up wrestling bears."

She grinned at the image that appeared

in her head. "I always thought it was the vodka."

"Hey, don't knock vodka," he said. "You'll wish we had some before this is all over."

MIKE FOLLOWED as she led the way. She knew the lay of the land better than he did. A lot more snow covered the ground here than on the Nome side, the buildings older and more weather-beaten, the place more of a village than a town. He followed her into the shadow of a warehouse-type brick building.

"This is as far as I've been," she said.

He nodded. They had a little better vantage point from here, the town spreading in front of them, smaller than he had expected, a few dozen buildings, no more. What had the smugglers done when they got to shore? Uelen hadn't been their original destination, he was fairly sure of that. They'd had a plane. Where had it been supposed to take them?

"How well do you know Siberia?" he asked.

"Not at all." Tessa shook her head.

"I'm thinking they are heading to Providenya. It's the closest airport. We have to head them off before they get there. Once they charter a plane, we'll never catch up."

"How far?"

"About sixty miles." He scanned the area again and spotted a small dark van on the other end of the harbor. Its windshield was free of snow. "I bet that belongs to our fishermen friends."

She nudged him around the corner of the building and nodded toward the three Kamaz trucks lined up in the back. "No need to go that far."

He flashed her a grin. "I like the way you think."

They made their way over carefully, watching for any danger. He brushed the snow off the driver's-side window and looked in. According to the red needle on the dashboard, the gas tank was almost full, plenty to get them where they were going. He cleaned off the windshield and the side mirror, Tessa already doing her share of the work on the other side.

Popping the lock posed little difficulty,

and hotwiring the truck was just as easy. He put it in reverse and pulled out, grinned. They were on their way.

He loved the chase, despite the inherent dangers of his job. He loved being on the road, going after the bad guys, making plans as he went, utilizing whatever happened to be at his disposal. There was such an adrenaline rush to it all, such a feeling of being alive, perhaps especially because not a single moment of his life was a given.

Maybe it was the Scottish blood in him, passed down by centurics of highland warriors.

"The adventure begins." He glanced over at her.

"With you, every day is an adventure," she said in a dry voice, but then smiled at him.

"I wouldn't trade it for a quiet ranch in Colorado if someone sweetened the deal with a cool million."

"Me, neither." She grinned. "We're both sick."

He stepped on the gas and bounced

down the pothole-ridden road with as much speed as he could, the rising sun behind them. "Let's catch us some warheads, honey."

"HOW FAR AHEAD of us do you think they are?" Tessa blinked her eyes to keep from falling asleep.

The heater was blowing warm air in her face, the radio tuned to a channel that aired Russian folk music, the only station that came in without static.

"Half a day, maybe. The man who'd brought them over said he had stopped on Big Diomede Island each way, which means their passage took longer. Handling and transporting the crates had to be cumbersome, too. I'm sure we're moving faster."

Another long silence nestled between them. It had been like this since the action had settled down. Probably both of them were feeling awkward about what had transpired in the dark recess of the cargo hold. She was, in any case.

"What happened on the boat—" Now

that they were out of immediate danger, she couldn't keep her mind from the unbidden passion that had erupted between them. "I don't know what to say."

"Then don't say anything. You're not going to overanalyze this, are you?" He flashed her a purely male look of long suffering.

"Yes, I am," she said, because perversely, annoying him made her feel better. She hated that she was more shaken by the experience than he was.

"We're still good together," he said.

The smug look of satisfaction on his face irritated her.

"That was never in question."

"What is, then?" He sounded exasperated.

"Whether or not we're good *for* each other."

"You're good for me."

"For your ego, you mean?" The muscles tightened in her neck. "Conquering the one that got away?"

"You don't get it. I don't want to conquer you, or dominate you, or keep you

in the kitchen barefoot and pregnant…"
He glanced at her. "I *have* fantasized about
you naked, but it wasn't confined to any
specific room of the house, or to the house
for that matter."

She smacked his shoulder. "See? You can't
even be serious about us for a moment."

"You have no idea how serious I am." His
gaze held hers until a pothole shook the
truck and he returned his attention to the
road.

"You wouldn't *mean* to take over, but
you wouldn't be able to help it. You're too
strong to do anything else." And she could
not live in the shadow of anyone; her independence was too dear to her, too hard-
won. She could never live the life her
mother lived.

"I'm not your father, Tess," he said in a
quiet voice. "And you're definitely not
your mother."

"I hate when you do that. When you use
something I shared in confidence and use
it to work against me."

"We are not working against each other."

"Aren't we?"

"We both want the same thing."

"Like you know what I want." *She* didn't even know what she wanted. Independence for sure. Love? More than anything, but could she have that without giving up the independence? To love would mean to have to trust, and trusting opened up a person for letdown and a world of hurt.

"I'm not like your father," he said again.

And he was right. He was nothing like her dad.

"What do I want, then?" she challenged him.

"To be happy. What's wrong with being happy together?"

"I want my own identity."

"What makes you think you would lose it?"

She took a deep breath. "Do you know what they used to call me on the base when someone couldn't remember my name?"

"Honey-buns?" A smile hovered over his lips.

"McNair's girl," she said. And they hadn't known the half of it, saying it only because Mike and she had been paired up for training.

"That's terrible."

"Right, like you think there's something wrong with that?"

"Not a damn thing. It sounds great. Awesome. But I'm sorry if it made you upset. You can keep your maiden name if it helps."

She opened her mouth, but her mind went blank so she closed it again.

"You want to marry me?" she asked after a few seconds, when she found her train of thought. The idea was so incredible, she could barely form the words. Was it possible that tough-guy, hell-raiser, playboy Mike McNair was—

"Where did you *think* we were going with this?" he asked, sounding offended.

Insane. They were going insane, both of them. She shook her head. "You just want me because you can't have me."

"I've just had you." He tapped his fingers on the steering wheel.

Heat rushed to her cheeks. "That's not

what I meant, and you know it. I'm probably the only woman who ever left you."

His silence confirmed her suspicions.

He focused on the road as he steered the truck over a patch of sheer ice. The highway wasn't much out here, the only thing distinguishing it from the rest of the snow-covered tundra were the parallel lines of piled-up snow and ice left behind by the last snowplow that had come this way—from the looks of it quite some time ago.

She was about to settle into pretend sleep, unwilling to continue this line of conversation, when she spotted the small dark dot on the horizon. "There."

He leaned forward over the steering wheel. "Too far to tell for sure." But he stepped on the gas a little harder, maneuvering to correct the slide of the tires, which had trouble sticking to the road despite the chain mesh that covered them.

In half an hour they were close enough to be able to tell that indeed it was another truck. An hour after that, they caught up and were preparing to pass it. The plowed strip was wide enough for one vehicle only, so they had to wait until they got to a spot where the wind had blown sufficient snow over the road to create a natural widening.

"Get down," Mike said.

"It's not your job to protect me."

"They know your face."

She slid down in her seat with a growl, hating that he was right.

"You hate it when I'm right, don't you?"

"The only thing I hate more is when you read my mind."

"Look now," he said after a few moments, and she straightened so she could catch a glimpse of them in the side-view mirror.

"Do you recognize them?" Mike drove on at the same speed.

"I think so."

"How many?"

"Four."

"That's what I counted. Didn't want to stare too hard."

"How far ahead should we get?"

"Fifteen to twenty miles. It will give us enough time to get ready to attack."

Chapter Ten

Mike kicked the tire that lay on the snow, shuffling to keep warm. Where the hell was the other truck? The gun smugglers should have caught up with them by now.

Maybe they had stopped to take a leak. Maybe they had a flat for real. He opened the door and hopped up into the cab. Might as well warm up for a little while. Stiff joints didn't make for good fighting.

Tessa was peering into the side-view mirror. "Can't believe they're not here yet."

He shrugged. "They'll come sooner or later. There's no other way." He took off his gloves to let in some warm air.

She riffled through the glove compartment, pulling out crunched up papers, screwdrivers, all kinds of junk. "Man, I'm hungry."

"Should have brought some ravioli." His stomach was tormenting him, too.

"Would you like some water?"

He glanced at the metal cup on the dashboard. They'd been melting snow in it. "I've had enough for now. You take it. It'll help fill up your stomach."

He watched her drink, the way her slim neck moved with every swallow. She had her parka on, but not her hood and gloves.

"Are you warm enough?"

She nodded.

They'd shut off the engine to conserve fuel, and without that the heater didn't work. It was cold in the cab, but not bad. At least they were out of the wind.

He slid to the middle of the wide bench seat next to her, where the steering wheel wasn't in his way and he could get comfortable.

An awkward silence stretched between them.

"It won't be long now," he said, having

no idea how long it would be, just wanting to say something.

"Mmm." She nodded.

Great.

"So you like the U.S.A.C.E.?"

"Not really. It's kind of boring."

Damn, but he loved that sexy voice of hers. The thought hit him out of nowhere. He shifted so their thighs touched. She didn't move away.

"How long did you stay with SF?" she asked.

"A year. Shorty and I were borrowed by the CIA for a special assignment at that point, and we ended up staying. Then I was recruited by yet another outfit after a while."

"Very mysterious." She wiggled her eyebrows. "I don't suppose you'd tell me who?"

He loved it when she was playful like this. "Not even under torture." He tried to look James Bondish.

"There are all kinds of torture, wouldn't you say?" She outlined his jaw with a slim finger.

She was right about that. His body tightened at her touch. He glanced at the side-view mirror. The road behind them was empty.

"You think you can make me talk?" A slow smile spread on his lips.

She lifted an eyebrow. "I think I can make you do just about anything." Her finger brushed over his lips.

He captured it with his mouth and bit it gently. He could get into this game.

"Does this team of yours have women in it?" She pulled her finger back but shifted her body closer.

He nodded. "As a matter of fact."

Interest sparked in her eyes. "Congressional policy notwithstanding?"

"They can't regulate something they have no knowledge of, now can they?" He smiled, seeing the wheels turn in her head.

"Ooh, I like that." She leaned forward until their cheeks touched. "Tell me more," she whispered into his ear.

His body was hard and ready. "Are we going somewhere with this or are you just teasing me?"

She closed her teeth over his earlobe for

a second. Then she said, "Harmless play, that's all."

He'd be the judge of that.

He captured her and pulled her onto his lap, unzipped her parka and pushed it off her shoulders. Instead of protesting, she shrugged it off the rest of the way.

She was slipping her fingers into his hair as he took her mouth. He kissed her long and slow, enjoying every soft moan, every brush of the tongue. Her cheeks looked flushed by the time he pulled back.

He dragged his gaze from her face to the side-view mirror. No truck in sight.

"Take off your boots."

Her eyes widened. "No."

"Chicken." He held her gaze as he reached over and turned the key in the ignition, bringing the heater to life.

She took a slow breath. Her mukluks fell to the floor with a thud.

"Your pants."

"Who made you boss?" She lifted her chin.

"Fine, I'll do it for you." And he did.

When she was naked, he arranged her

legs until she straddled him, and he ground his hard desire against her soft center.

"You're nuts," she said as her eyes glazed over. She didn't protest.

He glanced at the mirror again. They were still okay.

He unzipped his pants and shoved off his clothes to midthigh. The feel of her silky bottom on his skin sent him straining against her.

"I don't suppose this is going to be slow and languorous," she teased.

"Hard and fast," he said, gratified at the sound of her breath catching in her throat.

"What if I won't let you?" She was watching his face.

"I'm letting *you*." He leaned back. "Take me."

A quick predatory grin flashed over her features and she put her hands on his shoulders and pushed him into the seat further. She lifted her bottom and, without warning, slid down on him in one smooth glide, taking him into her moist heat fully.

He bit his lips as a small groan escaped

them, keeping one eye on the side-view mirror.

"I thought we said fast," he said when she stayed in place.

She lifted up and came down hard, slamming herself against him. The bolt of pleasure that shot up his body was blinding.

And she didn't stop.

He reached out to encircle her waist with his hands and sneaked his fingers up her hot skin under her layers of clothing. He could get as far as the underside of her breasts, but no further, damn it.

He gripped her rib cage as she rode him with abandon, stealing away his purpose, his very sanity. The energy between them was combustible, the heat scorching. They were fogging up the windows.

Glide, thrust, squeeze. Glide, thrust, squeeze. She was working him mercilessly.

He loved every second of it.

His body clenched tighter. He didn't bother holding back. This was what she wanted, to take his release from him. He gave it to her, shuddering, filling her with his seed as she still kept moving. Then she finally began to contract and squeezed him tighter still.

She arched her back and closed her eyes, and crumpled slowly against him.

He tried to catch his breath, breathing hard, caught a small movement in the mirror. She slid off him as soon as she felt him shift.

"Doesn't look like we're going to get to snuggle." He pulled up his pants and zipped his fly, trying to get his mind to come back to functioning from its shattered pieces. He watched the truck in the side-view mirror as it came closer and closer.

He slid over to the driver's seat, pulled his gloves back on and pushed his hood up. "I better get out there."

"Be careful."

"Caution is my middle name." He winked at her.

She gave him an impolite snort, still half-naked, reaching for her pants.

It was a sight worth memorizing.

He slammed the door shut behind him and narrowed his eyes against the cold wind. His body was warm, relaxed and limber. The men were closing on them, just a few hundred feet down the road now. They would have to stop. The Kamaz blocked the way.

He moved closer to the tire iron on the ground. The four men were probably armed to the teeth, while Tessa and he had one gun between them. He'd insisted that she keep it. His knife was a comforting weight in his pocket.

The truck drew closer, close enough now that he could see the displeasure and suspicion on the men's faces. They came to a slow halt, beeped the horn. He pointed at the tire he was changing and shrugged.

He took his sweet time, messing up and starting over several times, stopping to scrape ice off the metal with the tire iron. He didn't look up when he heard the other truck's door open.

The man's boots crunched the snow with each step as he came closer.

"Busted a tire," Mike looked at him at last when he was but a few feet away.

"Americanyetz," he yelled back to his truck. He was short but built like a tank, his face obscured by a scraggly beard. A rifle hung on his shoulder, within easy reach.

Another man jumped to the ground and came over. "What's going on?" This one was American, judging by both the way he talked and his clothing—a down ski jacket and matching pants, blue with white stripes. It looked funny with his AK-47.

"Having some trouble here," Mike said apologetically. "I'm not that handy. My partner is sick. I never realized how heavy these damned things were."

The man looked down both sides of the truck, no doubt measuring the ridges of snow and ice, calculating whether going around was possible or would get their vehicle stuck.

"We'll help," he said, apparently deciding to play it safe.

"I can't tell you how grateful I'd be. I'm Mike McDonald from Anchorage. The boss is a real hard-ass. I can't afford to be late with another delivery. You know what I mean?" He reached his hand for a handshake.

The man didn't take it. He was looking at the tire. "This one is no good either."

"Right. Of course. There's another one in the back if you can help me get it down." He went for the opening of the tarp and hauled himself up.

The American nodded to the Russian and sent him up.

"In the back." Mike let the tarp fall, enveloping them in darkness.

The Russian swore angrily.

Mike went for the spot where he'd seen the man's rifle, but didn't connect at once. "Sorry, let me get my flashlight." He fumbled around then his elbow hit against the butt of the gun and he grabbed for it, had the barrel shoved against the man's chest the next second. "Don't move."

The Russian lunged at Mike, but he brought the man down, his knee on the man's windpipe before he could raise a shout. They struggled for control of the gun. The man was strong and determined.

Mike doubled over when a fist slammed into his groin. Pain shot through his body. The Russian was going for the rifle. Mike put his full weight on his knee, still seeing stars as he heard the man's windpipe crush under the pressure. He held steady until all movement stopped.

"What the hell is taking so long?" The question came from outside.

He stood slowly, his teeth gritted together. "I think we're gonna need some help here." The pain and breathlessness in his voice sounded very much like someone who was straining to lift a heavy object, making it perfect for his purposes.

The man outside the canvas swore, something with "useless idiots" in it.

Mike slipped the rifle onto the dead man's shoulder and pulled him into a sitting position, just as the American parted the canvas and stepped up.

"What's going on?"

"I think he hurt his back." He slapped the Russian on the shoulder, waiting for the other one to drop the canvas so the two sitting in the cab of the truck behind them couldn't see what was going on.

Instead, the American lifted his gun. "Yurii?"

Mike stepped in front of the body and bent to grab the man's hands, started to pull him up. "Come on, buddy. I'll give you a hand." He closed his eyes, but could tell when the canvas dropped at last.

"He can handle it," the man said. "Let's take care of that damned tire."

Mike grabbed his knife, keeping his eyes closed for as long as possible, then opened them and went for the American. His eyes had less of an adjustment than the other man's whose had to go from light to dark, giving Mike a moment of advantage. It was all he needed. He buried the knife in the man's chest to the hilt. There. That one wasn't going to get up.

He waited, hoping the other two would come to investigate, but he waited in vain. He left the rifles, too big to hide and not much use to him anyhow. He couldn't very well be shooting at a truck that held nuclear weapons. All they needed was a bullet to hit the gas tank by accident.

He wiped off his knife on the man's coat and tucked it away, opened the canvas and jumped to the ground, waved to the two men before walking to the front of the Kamaz. He opened his door and sat next to Tessa.

"How's it going?"

"I took two out."

"Want me to try the other two?"

"They know your face." He shook his head. "They'd be shooting at you and you couldn't shoot back."

"Why the hell won't they get out?"

"They're smarter than they look, I suppose."

She rubbed the ridge of her nose, then dropped her hand and looked at him. "Remember those war games when we took the oil tanker?"

A second passed before he figured out what she was talking about. "Too dangerous. We're not playing with training lasers now."

"Got a better idea?"

Unfortunately, he didn't.

The truck behind them beeped its horn.

"You don't trust me."

"Of course I trust you."

"We're doing it then?" She tilted her head.

"Fine, we're doing it."

The scowl on her face turned into an excited smile as she threw herself into his arms and pressed her lips to his. He didn't need more invitation than that. Unfortunately, their situation didn't provide them with nearly enough time. He had to pull away all too soon.

"Be careful," he said, and turned off the motor.

She flashed him a cocky smile as she lifted her chin. "I'll be brilliant."

He slid out of the cab just as she was stashing the handgun in her parka's large pocket. He walked around the front, opened her door and tugged on her shoulder until her listless body fell into his arms. He let her down to the snow gently, making sure her hood covered as much of her face as possible, then hooked his hands under her arms and started to drag her toward the truck behind them.

The man on their side rolled his window down and yelled out, mostly swearwords, in Russian.

Mike paid no attention to him as he dragged Tessa on, keeping his body between the men and her. If they realized who she was too soon, things could go bad real fast. Then he was finally in line with the cab and turned, braced Tessa as she flipped back her hood with one hand and pulled the gun and aimed with the other. The men's momentary confusion was enough. She squeezed off two shots in quick succession before they realized what was going on, both bullets hitting their aim.

She jumped up and winked at him. "What did I tell you?" She strutted just a little as she went to the back of the truck and pulled aside the canvas. "What the hell?"

He pulled his gun. Were there more men in the back? Had they picked up help at Uelen?

But when he got next to her, he didn't find anyone else. He didn't find anything at all. The truck was empty.

"WHERE DID THE CRATES GO?"

The stunned look on Mike's face was so out of character, Tessa would have laughed if she wasn't so bewildered herself.

"They must have made the drop already."

"Where? When?"

"After we passed them." Mike kicked the license plate. "Maybe they never meant to take the load to Providenya. There has to be police there, some army. Security, in any case—they have an airport."

"Maybe they just wanted the warheads out of Uelen, away from the port authority, looking for a quiet spot to make a transfer." She finished the thought for him.

"Right. They don't need to go to the airport to rendezvous with a plane. A snow plane can land on any flat stretch of snow, provided it's frozen enough. Or they could be passing the goods on to a chopper."

"But we haven't heard anything." Noise traveled far over the thick silence of the frozen tundra, and anything that came from Providenya would have flown almost directly overhead.

"What if it's not a direct exchange, for confidentiality's sake? The guys who brought the warheads might not know who the customer is. The deal is between two bosses—the delivery and pickup crew don't meet face to face."

He was making a hell of a lot of sense. "So they dropped the crates at a prearranged location and called in the drop."

He nodded. "Can't be more than a few miles from here. If they had the pickup plane waiting in Providenya, it would take a while to get here after they received the call that the goods were dropped." He was already running for the cab.

She was right behind him. She yanked the body out of the seat the same time he did on the other side, then they were in and he had the motor started, backing down the road with just as much speed as they dared to go. There was no room to turn around.

"If they covered the crates with snow, we might miss them," she thought out loud.

"They couldn't have covered them. They would want the chopper to find them."

"They might have had some kind of a beacon." She was taking off her seat belt already, opening the sliding window that separated the cab from the back of the truck. "I'll watch for anything out of place," she said as she climbed through.

She had to hang on to the metal ribs of the side, but made her way quickly to the end. Sitting above the taillights with the canvas pulled back was no picnic. The freezing air blew into her face so hard she could only open her eyes to a slit. Still, it was sufficient.

She watched the accumulated snow ridges on each side, waiting to see where they were knocked down. She hugged her arms around her body. Her face was going numb. Nothing. Maybe the men had left the crates at Uelen. She was about to get up to talk to Mike about it when they came to where the wind had blown enough snow across the road to level it with the rest of the land, the same spot where they had passed the smugglers an hour or so before.

She yelled back, then got up and ran to the open window as the truck was already slowing. "This is it."

"Figures. Easier to push the crates on

the snow then trying to lift them over the snow bank." Mike shut off the engine.

She went back to the tailgate and jumped off.

"This way." He was already following the tracks.

The smugglers hadn't hidden the crates, after all, they were sitting in an indentation of snowdrifts, not something someone would have caught driving down the road if he wasn't looking, but in plain sight of anyone from above.

There were four.

"Brady," Mike said. "He must have been in the chopper that took the crate from the dog sled."

"And he gave it right back to the smugglers. I'll bring the truck over," she said, and made a run for it.

By the time she backed up to the crates, Mike had already pushed one from the rest.

"It's gonna be heavy," he said, stating the obvious.

They tried anyway.

She lifted until she thought her eyes

would pop out, but they couldn't get the crate onto the truck bed. It had probably taken all four men to lower it, an easier task than lifting the thing up with gravity working against them.

"Damn it." She jumped back as her end of the crate slipped from her fingers and slammed into the snow.

She looked up and scanned the empty sky. They still had time. She bent again, wiggled her fingers under the crate in the snow, and when Mike gave the word, put all her strength into the lift. They made it up to elbow height, but at that point they had to switch from lifting to pushing up, a transition they couldn't make. The crate slammed into the snow a second time.

Defeat tasted bitter in her mouth. Until this moment she hadn't given failing much thought; now it seemed inevitable. "Try the phone again."

He did. "Still not working."

"Wait a minute." She looked back down the road from where they'd just come. "If the smugglers made arrangements for the crates to be picked up, they must have had some access to communications."

"Good thinking. I'm going back to search the bodies. Are you coming or staying?"

"Staying. In case anybody shows up here."

He stepped up to the cab and tossed her one of the rifles. "You still got the handgun?"

She nodded. "Hurry back."

"Count on it," he said before he closed the door and drove away.

He was going just fifteen miles down the road. Nothing to worry about. She stomped her feet to keep warm. When they were done here, she was going to find the nearest hot tub, crawl into it and forget to come out.

She walked around the crates absentmindedly, listening for the sounds of a motor nearing, be it from the road or the sky. She stopped as something caught her attention. The crate in the back was shaped slightly differently than the other three. Interesting.

All four crates were unmarked, looking the same other than the small difference in the size of one. Did that signify anything? Were the contents different?

She tried to pry off the lid, but without success, and resisted the temptation to wedge the rifle's barrel under the edge for extra leverage. Bending the barrel was not a good idea. She needed the gun to keep its true aim. Their lives could depend on it.

She kicked the edge of the top instead with full force, and regretted it instantly as she hopped back on one foot. That had been stupid. Mukluks were great to keep one's feet warm, but they were a poor substitute for steel-toed boots.

She sat on the crate and took a deep breath. She was getting cold. The heat Mike and she had generated between them had left her body, although certain parts were still lingering pleasantly over certain memories. She smiled. He'd been right. They *were* good together.

The admission came easier than she'd thought. And there was a second one, coming right after the first. She was still in love with him.

She took a moment and let the shock abate.

She was in love with Mike McNair.

What on earth was she going to do about it?

The choices were limited. She could either ignore her feelings or go with them. She had run from him once; she would be damned if she ran again.

He had hinted at marriage, but hadn't said anything about love. Not that it meant he didn't love her necessarily. He was a man, after all. They did tend to focus on the goal and didn't much dwell on feelings.

And if he loved her, then what?

He damn well better get down and propose as if he meant it. She was having no part in some military-style marital hijacking. She wanted romance, a clear profession of love and words of tenderness.

She shifted and the crate creaked under her. She scooted aside to look at the boards, wiggled them. One was a little loose. She slid off the crate and yanked the board around some more, and after a while it gave.

The gap was enough to squeeze in one

hand. There were rows and rows of smaller boxes stacked under some fluffy packing material. She grabbed one, but it was too big to pull out. She pushed the packing aside, pulled her hand out so she could see in. *A plain box. Great.* Then she caught a red line on the corner. She pushed more stuffing out of the way, and her heart about stopped. She was standing next to a crate of TNT.

And that was not the worst news. Tessa looked up at the sound of an approaching chopper.

"SHORTY," MIKE BARKED into the phone, driving the truck in reverse with one hand. "Where the hell are you? I need you, buddy."

"Mike?"

"I'm on the road between Uelen and Providenya, about sixty miles out of Uelen. We got what we came for. We need pick up. Badly."

"Are you all right?"

"Not for long, if you're not coming. Their pick up is probably on the way. It's all down to who'll get here first. Are you at the hangars?" He could hear the noise of a chopper through the phone.

"Yeah. It'll take me just a minute to take off. I already had clearance for a different destination. Hang in there. I'll be there before you know it. Trust me."

"Thanks. I owe you one."

They clicked off at the same time. He tossed the phone aside, put both hands on the steering wheel and stepped up his speed.

He saw them from his side-view mirror first, a Russian Hip, Mi-8 helicopter, already landed with the blades still turning, two men in white Arctic overalls on the ground, both with their rifles aimed at Tessa, who was holding them off.

The pilot was still in his seat. Didn't look like he was getting involved. A hired man most likely. Good.

Mike tore down the road, ignoring the gunfire one of the men opened on him. He was out of the truck a split second after the engine was shut off. He stayed in the cover of the vehicle, took a quick look, enough to see that Tessa had taken cover behind one of the crates.

How long could they hold out? The men had automatic weapons, while he and Tessa had old rifles with a few bullets each. Shorty was never going to get to them in time.

Chapter Eleven

Mike shot at the men, forcing them to the ground. He was prepared to do whatever it took to keep Tessa safe for as long as possible.

Some of his bullets must have hit uncomfortably close to the chopper because it lifted up, circled above them a couple of times, then landed again on the road in front of the truck, out of the line of fire.

Mike ducked as the side of the truck got sprayed with bullets. Damn it. He had to move. If they hit the gas tank he'd be blown sky-high. And that was just what they were trying to do.

He threw himself into the snow and crawled on his stomach using for cover any indentation he could find. He needed to get behind Tessa, who was covering him as best she could. How long before she ran out of bullets?

For now, the attackers left her alone, being careful with the warheads, and concentrated on him. He had to duck and keep his head down. The shots came steadily. Not much of a chance to answer, except when Tessa kept the men flattened to the snow, but then their white Arctic overalls made them nearly invisible.

Still, he managed to take one out. The other, feeling his own doom, now that he was outnumbered, started to shoot indiscriminately at Tessa and the crates. Tessa pulled down, tossed her rifle aside. She was out of bullets. She pulled her pistol, managed to wound the guy, but it didn't slow him down any. He knew now that he was going to die. He advanced forward with the kind of bravado only men who have nothing to lose tended to have.

Then Tessa was out of bullets altogether, and Mike in the worst possible position with her and the crates between him and the attacker. He crawled to the side. He had to get to a spot from where he could take a good shot without risking her life. He discarded his right glove, wanting to make sure nothing could mess up the next shot, the only one he might get. The metal of the trigger was so cold it burned his skin, his finger stiff from the frigid temperature before he got more than a couple of yards.

Then a shot came from his right and he rolled before he realized it hadn't been aimed at him. The man on the other side of the crates fell silent. The pilot had taken him out.

What the hell? He looked for the man and spotted him just in time as he jumped from behind a snowbank and rushed to Tessa's side.

His body, the way he moved, seemed familiar.

Then he took off his helmet.

"Shorty?"

Mike came to his knees, then pushed to his feet, staring at the man. "How the hell did you get here?"

Shorty raised his pistol to Tessa. "As soon

as I heard it was you those idiots took, I knew there would be trouble," he said to her.

No! Not now when they were so close to having made it, damn it. Mike held his grip on the rifle tight as hot fury washed through him, mixed with a staggering sense of betrayal. He held back the over-whelming urge to charge at the man and let the bullets fly where they may. He couldn't put Tessa in any more danger than she already was. The sight of the gun pressed to her skin made his heartbeat slow.

He loved her. *Hell of a time to realize it now.*

He wasn't going to let anything happen to her, that was for damned sure.

He kept his eyes on Shorty. "I thought I knew you."

"You do." The asshole grinned. "Haven't you always said I was the craziest bastard you ever met?"

He nodded. Yes, he'd said that enough, jokingly. Shorty had pulled his share of stunts over the years. "Not this crazy."

The man shrugged.

"I can't believe you would hook up with Brady." He made an effort to talk friendly and keep the rage out of his voice. He measured the distance carefully between them. *Too wide to cover in a single jump.*

"We've always worked good together." Shorty grinned.

Always? The words slammed into Mike with a physical force. The memory of how Shorty had begged him not to turn the man in. "He never had anything on you, did he?"

Shorty shook his head. "We were running that little business together."

The betrayal stung. "I thought we were friends."

Shorty shrugged. "That weekend in Vegas with the guys? I lost more than I let on."

He had to get over it. He had to get his mind off the past and into the present, find a way to stop this insanity. "How about now? Did Brady convince you this was some noble fight against an old enemy who hasn't lost all his teeth yet?"

Shorty sneered at him. "This time around I'm the boss. Brady did what I told him." He looked between Tessa and Mike. "I must say, he did disappoint me."

"At least you can be certain that won't happen again," Tessa said, her voice clipped with anger.

Shorty raised his eyebrow. "So that's how it went down? The old boy is out?"

Mike nodded.

Shorty didn't seem bothered. "Come on, now," he said to Mike. "Don't look at me like that. You never had a head for business. You can't be mad at me because I have."

Mike kept his fury in check. "Have you thought about how many people are going to die? Women and children. Can you live with that?"

"I'm pushing no buttons. Besides, nuclear weapons don't kill people. People kill people."

"It's not a joke, damn it." He heard his voice rise and took it down a notch. He could not lose his cool now. "It's not worth it, man. If it's money you need, let's talk about it. We were friends once. I'll help."

"Not with this stuff." Shorty shook his head.

Was that a hint of wistfulness in his voice?

"How about Vicky and the kids? This is going to come out sooner or later. Think of what it will do to them."

"I'm leaving them taken care of. I'm not cut out for marriage, anyway. Should have never done it." His face turned hard and serious. "I'm in trouble with the wrong people this time. I have to leave the country and I can't ever come back. I need enough money to last the rest of my life."

"We were friends once. You said I could trust you."

"I lied."

What was wrong with Tessa's eye? She was blinking like a semaphore. Mike nodded as if to Shorty's last words, letting Tessa know she had his attention.

She looked at his rifle then back into his eyes, to the rifle then to him again. What did she want? He couldn't toss her the gun, and he couldn't lift it, aim it and shoot Shorty, not when all the man had to do was pull the trigger and Tessa would be dead.

"So what now?" he asked.

"Now you help me load the crates and I won't shoot either of you. I'm gonna have to take out the truck, however."

Mike shrugged. "Leaving us alive won't be much use then, will it? The weather will kill us, anyway." He was talking only to stall for time. Shorty meant to kill them. He had no doubt about that.

"Maybe. Then again, you always were a crafty bastard. No telling what you'll come up with."

"Leave us the truck."

Shorty laughed. "You're in no position to negotiate."

"And if I don't help you?"

"I'll shoot your girlfriend."

"You touch her, I rip your throat out."

"That's nice. Consider this, though. I either fly out of here with the crates or blow them up right here. I'm not going to prison. And if I have to bite the dust— well, snow—you two will be biting it with me." He paused. "Let's see, where is the wind blowing from? The west. Too bad for the people of Alaska."

"It would take more than that pistol to set off those warheads."

"How about 150 pounds of TNT?"

It was his turn to sneer. "That would work if you had it."

"He does," Tessa said quietly and nodded toward one of the crates.

Oh, hell.

"I know." Shorty flashed him a superior grin. "It's not smart to transport it together with the other stuff, but what can I do? It was on the purchase order."

Tessa blinked three times, slowly. One. Two. Three. Then she moved her feet a little.

She was getting ready to do something. On the count of three. He nodded again, as if to Shorty.

She blinked. One. Two. Three. She threw herself to the ground at the same time as Mike raised his gun. Shorty squeezed off a shot, but it missed her, she was already gone. Then the pistol was aimed at Mike. He returned fire, jerking the rifle barrel up a second later as Tessa jumped into the picture.

She threw herself on Shorty from the side, catching him unaware. Her first kick sent the pistol flying, the second broke Shorty's jaw with a sickening crunch. The man howled as he rolled on the ground, making it hard to wedge the rifle barrel under his chin, but Mike managed.

Tessa had the pistol by then, holding it on the man. "All right, stop the drama. It's just a broken bone," she said.

Mike glanced at her. Damn she was tough. He picked up his glove and pulled it on. Couldn't afford to get frostbite now. He was planning on doing some serious fondling at the earliest opportunity.

"Okay, this is how it's gonna go," he said to Shorty as he pulled him up. "You help me load the crates into the chopper, and I'll leave you here with the truck."

Shorty shook his head.

"If you don't help, I'll break your nose. We can keep going in that direction for a while. There are a lot of ways to hurt a man without impairing his ability to lift."

Hate burned in Shorty's eyes, but he nodded.

Mike handed his rifle to Tessa. "I'll bring over the chopper. If he as much as blinks the wrong way, shoot him."

"With pleasure," she said, and smiled.

SHORTY WAS TALKING with his broken jaw, his words barely intelligible. Something that resembled "you take out Mike and I'll take you with me" and another couple of words about lots of money.

"I never really liked you that much. Don't push your luck," Tessa said.

Come to think of it, this wasn't the first time he'd tried to come between her and Mike. At the hotel three years ago when she had walked in on them, he could have explained the two women belonged to him. He could have backed Mike up. Instead he had grinned at her like the jackass she now knew he was.

She drew up her shoulders against the swirling snow as the chopper set down next to the crates. Mike jumped out.

"Okay, let's do it. Remember, buddy, we are both armed and you're not. You drop the crate, you're dead."

Mike slung the rifle over his shoulder, and Tessa did the same with hers. They grabbed the first crate, staggering under the weight. Shorty seemed to have taken Mike's words to heart because he was lifting his share.

She was glad Mike had found a way to force him to help, but she didn't feel comfortable leaving Shorty behind. He would have little choice but to go back to the evil work he had given himself to. Someday, somewhere he would pop up again. And he would do damage. She would have to talk to Mike about that.

They loaded the first crate without trouble, then the second and the third. They left the explosives for last. It was a smaller crate and went a little easier than the warheads. Then they were done, and before she could blink, Mike had Shorty on the ground on his stomach, his hands behind his back, in the process of getting tied together. When did he get the rope?

"You baftard. You faid you'll leave me." Shorty raged against Mike as he lifted him up and tossed him after the crates.

Mike shrugged. "I lied."

THE CHOPPER FLEW over the icy waters of the Bering Sea.

"You know, this was fun." Tessa leaned back in her seat. Relief softened her muscles, but she wasn't tired. If anything, she was energized.

Mike glanced over and shook his head. "You shaved ten years off my life."

"You need to learn to relax."

"I'd have to be dead to feel relaxed around you."

"Ahh, do I make you nervous?"

"Very." But he shook his head. "With the stuff you get into—I live in constant fear for your life."

"Didn't seem like you worried too much over me in the last couple of years."

"I forgot how crazy you were."

"Yeah. I bet you forgot all about me."

He held her gaze. "I remembered plenty."

The heat that radiated from him made her squirm in her seat.

"I suppose you're going to want some big ridiculous church wedding and make me wear a bow tie," he said.

"It would be nice to be asked." She drew herself up in her seat.

"You know I can't ask you, Tessa. You'd say no just for the sake of fighting."

"So you figure your best chance is to try and bully me into it?"

"Pretty much."

"I hope you have a backup plan."

"Don't I always?" He flashed her a cocky smile. "If bullying doesn't work, I'm gonna seduce you and try to get a yes out of you in the throes of passion."

The hours they'd spent on the boat flashed through her mind, making her body tingle.

"Come to think of it," he said, "I'll do the seducing anyway. For good measure."

"I never took you for the marrying type."

"You changed me."

Did she? Could she truly believe him? Could she risk her heart? She had to, didn't she? Because the only other alternative was not having him in her life, and that she couldn't bear.

"Why do you want to marry me?"

He shook his head. "I knew you were

going to make me do all the mushy stuff just to see me squirm. Take over the joystick."

She did, her heart flipping over in her chest when he took off his seat belt and went down on one knee as much as the room in the cockpit allowed.

Shorty said something in the back, the words unintelligible, his tone full of derision.

"Excuse me for a moment." Mike stood and grabbed a glove.

There was some groaning in the back.

"Now, where were we," he said when he came back and took up the position again.

"I want to marry you because you are the most amazing person I have ever known. Because the past three years were hell without you. Because you're brave and strong and sexy and I am nuts about you. Tessa Nielsen, I love you, and I am going to keep on loving you for the rest of my life. Would you please just this once not be pigheaded and agree to be my wife?"

He took her hand, but she pulled it back.

"You were doing good until that last sentence."

"Okay, let me try again. Would you please put me out of my misery and agree to be my wife?" He put on a roguish expression. "Will ye be my bonnie bride, lass?"

That sexy brogue just about did her in. "And you'll be reasonable?"

"Yes."

"I'm going to try to get into whatever group it is you're working for. Are you going to have a problem with that?"

Her military career had started out of a desire to learn how to be strong and wanting to follow in her brother's footsteps, but down the line it had turned into something more. She enjoyed it and she was good at it. She liked the feeling of making a difference. "I'm not kidding, Mike. I'm not quitting so you can take care of me and satisfy some deep-seated macho need."

"I'll give you a reference. I'll put in a recommendation."

"Okay, hypothetical question. We are

home and it's the middle of the night. We hear a burglar downstairs. Are you going to lock me in the bedroom, or are you going to let me go downstairs and beat up his sorry ass?"

"Can we go together?"

She thought for a moment. "Deal."

"Is that a yes?"

"Yes, that's a yes." The fight went out of her. She had trouble catching her breath. "I love you, don't you know that?" She had never stopped loving him.

He held her gaze. "God, I would have given anything to hear you say that. There was a time when I was scared to death you wouldn't."

She smiled.

"A word of warning," he said, and she stiffened.

"Grandpa Fergus will likely want to play the bagpipe at the wedding. He'd be hurt if we said no. I'm probably going to have to get married in a kilt."

She let out a slow breath and savored the image that came to mind. "I can live with that."

"I'm dying to kiss you." He leaned closer. "What's keeping you?"

"The fear of crashing." He grinned.

"See? That's the kind of stuff I'm talking about. If we are going to get married, you are going to have to put a lot more faith in me. I'll have you know, I'm an excellent pilot."

"In you, I have all the faith in the world," he said and closed the distance between them.

Epilogue

"I can't believe we're working undercover on our honeymoon. How could you agree to this?" Mike shook his head.

"It's just surveillance," Tessa said and smoothed some more suntan lotion over her legs.

He swallowed, his mouth feeling dry as he watched her slim fingers glide over her calves and up to her thighs. They were stretched out on a private beach in Venezuela, the favorite hangout of Paolo Sanchez, a major international financier who had been linked recently to a certain terrorist group.

"I wonder how Sasha is doing?"

"Probably gained ten pounds by now, knowing Kelly," he said.

His youngest sister adored the dog and had begged for the job of dog-sitting. The other huskies had been taken back into service by the U.S.A.C.E. Tessa had insisted on Sasha's discharge and adoption.

He had a wife, a house and a dog. If that wasn't the most freakishly normal thing he'd done in his adult life, he didn't know what was. He loved it.

Dave walked by without looking at either of them, his large footprints following him in a neat row on the wet sand. The surf broke against the beach with a musical sound. The air was filled with the smell of salt water, the breeze bringing a whiff of suntan lotion now and then.

"Guess our shift is over." Mike sat up.

Tessa followed Dave with her eyes without turning her head. "That man needs a good waxing."

Mike flinched. "I wouldn't mention that to him if I were you."

"When would I have a chance to talk to your friends? You don't let me near them."

"We're not supposed to know them. And even if we weren't undercover, I wouldn't want any of them within a mile of you. It's our honeymoon." He picked up his towel and tossed it over his shoulder as he glanced down the length of the beach. Other than Dave Reyburn, he couldn't spot anyone from the team, although there had to be at least one more man watching. They were taking shifts in twos.

"You worry about Dave seducing me?" She grinned at him.

"No." Not Dave. Short and bulky and covered in hair in the most unattractive places, Dave Reyburn was hardly a ladies' man. But some of the others were. He'd almost had to punch Eric's lights out the night before for staring at Tessa half the night at the bar.

"Thanks for the vote of confidence." She gathered up her belongings and drew a finger down his arm, instantly setting his body on full alert. "There is only one man I'm interested in."

He grinned, loving the sound of that.

"Pepito, the chef," she said.

She turned, but he grabbed after her and pulled her to him, wiped the mischievous smile off her lips with his own. He kissed her longer and harder than he meant to. He could never quite get enough.

"You hungry?" He asked when he pulled away.

"Mmmm?"

"Pepito." He rubbed the stubble of his cheek against the soft skin on her neck.

"Pepito who?"

"That's what I thought." He swung her into his arms. "We'll get room service."

"I like a man who knows how to take charge," she said against his neck.

"Since when? Don't you go changing on me now." He balanced her with one hand as he opened the door. Their bungalow was right on the beach.

"I'm not saying I want you to be bossing me around all the time." She slid her feet to the ground, and before he knew what was going on, she had one leg stuck behind his, a sudden tug at his elbow sending him onto the bed on his back.

"I do like to get my turn," she said, already straddling him.

He reached up and pulled her down for

a kiss that left both of them panting. He slid a hand down her back and came away with her bikini top, then used her momentary pause to flip them and pin her under him.

"Are we going to spend the rest of our lives wrestling for control?" she asked as she slipped a hand between them and cupped him.

"Probably." He formed the single word with concentration as he lowered his lips to a rosy nipple.

"You know, I kind of like it this way." She locked her legs around his hips.

"Me, too," was the last thing he said before he descended on his target.

* * * * *

Don't miss Dana Marton's next gripping tale of romantic suspense! Look for PROTECTIVE MEASURES, featuring the SDDU, coming in May 2006.

HARLEQUIN®
INTRIGUE®

WE'LL LEAVE YOU BREATHLESS!

If you've been looking for thrilling tales of
contemporary passion and sensuous love stories
with taut, edge-of-the-seat suspense—then
you'll love Harlequin Intrigue!

Every month, you'll meet six new heroes
who are guaranteed to make your spine tingle
and your pulse pound. With them you'll enter
into the exciting world of Harlequin Intrigue—
where your life is on the line
and so is your heart!

THAT'S INTRIGUE—
ROMANTIC SUSPENSE
AT ITS BEST!

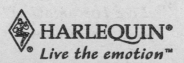

HARLEQUIN®
Live the emotion™

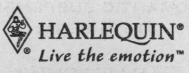

Harlequin Historicals®
Historical Romantic Adventure!

From rugged lawmen and valiant knights to defiant heiresses and spirited frontierswomen, Harlequin Historicals will capture your imagination with their dramatic scope, passion and adventure.

Harlequin Historicals . . . they're too good to miss!

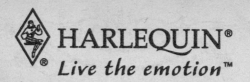
HARLEQUIN®
Live the emotion™

Upbeat,
All-American Romances

Romantic Comedy

 Harlequin Historicals®
Historical,
Romantic Adventure

INTRIGUE
Romantic Suspense

HARLEQUIN ROMANCE®
The essence of
modern romance

HARLEQUIN®
Presents
Seduction and passion
guaranteed

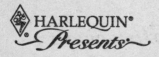
Emotional,
Exciting, Unexpected

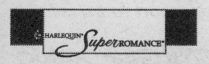

Sassy, Sexy, Seductive!

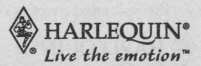

HARLEQUIN®
Presents

The world's bestselling romance series...
The series that brings you your favorite authors,
month after month:

Helen Bianchin...Emma Darcy
Lynne Graham...Penny Jordan
Miranda Lee...Sandra Marton
Anne Mather...Carole Mortimer
Susan Napier...Michelle Reid

and many more uniquely talented authors!

Wealthy, powerful, gorgeous men...
Women who have feelings just like your own...
The stories you love, set in exotic, glamorous locations...

HARLEQUIN®
Presents

Seduction and Passion Guaranteed!

HPDIR104